SYNNR'S KISS

KATE RUDOLPH

ABOUT SYNNR'S KISS

There's no going back from abduction…

Luci hates that most of her friends see her as fragile and in need of protection, rather than the strong woman she's growing into. Everyone but Ax, that is. She doesn't want a relationship. But she's more than happy to spend her time with the gorgeous warrior until unexpected intrigue forces them closer than ever.

Ax will protect his Match…

Luci owns Ax's heart before he realizes he's given it to her, but telling her that may send her running. When they're stuck together on an unplanned journey, Ax will do everything it takes to keep his mate safe. But she's stronger than she looks and she's not about to let Apsyns torture her… again.

As danger swirls around them, so do the intense emotions they've been avoiding. To get back home they'll need to rely on each other, but facing their feelings may be even more frightening than fighting the Apsyns determined to end them.

Luci: It's really sexy when you flare your wings like that. Do you ever use them when...

Ax: When what?

Luci: When you're being intimate.

THE SCENT of danger hung in the air as Axitzar Sube breathed deep. Kilrym was dark tonight. Its moon, Aorsa, wouldn't give up any light during this war.

No. Ax was too poetic. The Synnrs of Aorsa cared about the light; the moon itself was dark by nature and had a moon cycle that paid no attention to wars and kingdoms.

And Ax didn't have time to think more about that. He stood on a rooftop and looked down at the streetlights below him. It was quiet out, but the promise of violence was heavy in every breath he took.

Something thumped behind him and he spun, wings out and his spark ready to shoot.

An Apsyn in body armor with gigantic purple wings made of electricity flared out to their fullest stood in an attack stance behind him. The Apsyn didn't give Ax time to do anything but fight.

Ax was clumsy as a blast of electricity hit him on the arm. He knew how to do this. He had been playing with his spark for years and years. But now he had to target the soldier, not play like a boy. The spark was intrinsic to all Zulir, but he still needed to practice.

He channeled his power in front of him in a strong blast that sent the Apsyn flying back and tumbling off the edge of the roof. Good. They couldn't quite use their wings to fly, so even if the Apsyn survived he would need to climb the seven stories of the building to get back up.

But Ax didn't have a moment to rest. A second Apsyn appeared, followed quickly by a third. They traded blows and blasts, and Ax managed to hit one of them with a critical shot before the second one hit him. Ax stumbled back to his own portion of the ledge, arms flailing to keep his balance as his feet scuttled against loose gravel.

He managed to put up a shield at the last minute to stop more blasts from taking him out, but this Apsyn wouldn't stop, and Ax didn't have any backup coming. He was cornered and out of options.

He looked around frantically, hoping for some sort of way out of the situation, but that wasn't going to happen.

Ax tipped backwards, wings flaring wide to guide the fall. But as he began to soar downwards, the blast of the enemy Apsyn's spark ripped through him. Ax screamed in pain and lost his concentration and his hold on his wings as they dissolved and let him free fall seven stories down to the dingy street.

Before Ax could hit the ground, the hologram dissolved around him.

Ax wasn't free falling off of a roof on Kilrym. He was standing in a military facility in the city of Osais on Aorsa, the moon of Kilrym, and training for the war that was already raging.

Solan Zadra stood at the edge of the hologram field, arms crossed and a sour look on his face. "Did you want to commit suicide? Or were you hoping to magically gain the ability to teleport?" he asked before grabbing a towel and tossing it to Ax. The light caught on Solan's new mating tattoo, the design carefully integrated with the tattoo he'd had before meeting his Match.

Ax wiped some of the sweat off of himself and swung his arms around to stretch his bunched up muscles. "It wasn't like I had another option," he said in his own defense. He only had so much power in his spark. And he doubted that the Apsyns would have stopped coming. What was the point of wings if they couldn't jump off a building every so often?

Solan didn't like his excuse. "We train so you can learn to spot other options."

"Do you really think we'll have that much time to think when we're out in the field?" Ax hated that he sounded young. It had only been six months since his first mission, and at twenty-three, he was one of the younger soldiers in Solan's unit. But he had been deemed incredibly intelligent in the Military Academy, and Ax hated that it didn't seem to transfer over so easily to the field.

"You learn to adapt if you want to survive," Solan warned before dismissing Ax and letting him go to the locker room.

Ax changed out of his training clothes and headed for the shower, where he stood for several extra minutes, letting the scalding water wash away some of the shame of a failed training session. He wanted to succeed.

He wanted to prove that he could do this and make his people proud as they fought this war. The Apsyns and Synnrs had been fighting all of his life in one form or another, and he doubted it would ever stop. But this was his opportunity to make his mark.

The water started to run cold and Ax stepped out of it. He put on his uniform and glanced at his communicator to see that he was being summoned to Major Ozar's office. She was in charge of the training facility and handed out assignments to test young soldiers. She also sent them to remedial training.

But Ax tried not to think about *that*.

Solan would have mentioned if he thought Ax was at risk of being sent away. One failed training session wasn't enough to doom him.

Ax was doing fine. He kept telling himself that as he walked down the narrow hallways of the training facility and into the wider hallways of the officer's offices. Major Ozar's office was bright, a giant window taking up one of the walls and looking out over the city. She sat behind her desk and was looking at a folder when he came in. She nodded for him to take a seat and he did, waiting quietly for her to acknowledge him.

"Why haven't you put in your genetic material into the Matching database?" she asked, setting the folder down and fixing him with a targeted glare.

That wasn't the question that Ax had expected. And he wasn't sure what he was supposed to say. It wasn't a requirement to serve in the military, but most soldiers wanted Matches and scoured the database for potential mates.

Matched units went farther than single soldiers. But Ax wasn't sure he was ready to be tied down with a Matched partner for life. It was more of a commitment than he was ready for. But he couldn't tell that to his boss. He scrambled for something to say. "It's…"

"None of my business," Major Ozar cut him off, and Ax could not have been more thankful. He really had no idea what was about to come out of his mouth. She slid the folder across her desk. "You have a new assignment. And I want you to think about Matching because we're going to need all of the power we can get." It sounded like a suggestion rather than an order, but it was hard to decipher the truth when it came from the major.

But she was right. Matched pairs were much stronger than single soldiers, and that's why they rose so quickly in the ranks. "You think battle is coming?" War had officially been declared when the Apsyns attacked the Synnr queen during a peace summit. But when Apsyns lived on a planet and Synnrs lived on its moon, there was no obvious battlefield from which to launch hostilities.

"Of course not." But Major Ozar's words were not a comfort. "This war will be fought on every front."

This was going to be a war of subterfuge and

sabotage, of fights they wouldn't see coming and had little hope to stand against. She was right. They were going to need every bit of power that they could find.

"Look over at the assignment and report there in the morning," Major Ozar told him. And then he was dismissed.

Ax had a lot to think about.

Maybe it was time to find a Match.

LUCI BURKE WAS TRYING her best to not be intimidated.

It wasn't working.

The University of Aorsa was the most prestigious college on the moon, and many Synnrs got the best education possible there. She'd been accepted and was now ready to start college just like so many normal nineteen-year-olds back on Earth.

Normal. Right. What a joke.

Luci couldn't call herself normal at all. Not after being abducted by aliens and forcibly experimented on for months. She'd been rescued six months before, but the nightmares persisted. Nightmares a *normal* nineteen-year-old couldn't begin to imagine.

Luci took a deep breath and tried not to think about that. She was safe. She wasn't at risk from any Apsyns finding her again. At least she hoped not.

Sometimes her nightmares told her otherwise. Sometimes she dreamed about being stuck in that lab once more as the Apsyns tried to dissect her and figure out what it meant to be human on a molecular level.

Those Apsyns were dead. She was safe.

And she was going to college.

She lived among the humans who had also been rescued from the Apsyns, and she was the first one to try college. Looking around at all of the people walking across campus, Luci was relieved to see that she wasn't the only human there, but none of them were her friends.

Emily, Lena, and Zac were all making their own paths by falling for Synnr warriors. And now all three of them had entered the military in one form or another and were ready to fight the Apsyns in the inevitable war that Luci was sure would wreck what little peace she'd managed to salvage.

Some of the others had gotten jobs in Osais, but Crowze, a Synnr soldier and one of Zac's mates, had ensured that none of them needed to work for their meals. They had time to heal.

Thanks to him, Luci had her spot at the university.

She had passed all the tests. Thanks to a translation implant, she could read and write in the Zulir language. But Aorsa wasn't Earth, and Luci was keenly aware of every difference. Even the tutor Crowze had hired to help her pass the entrance exams couldn't make up for a lifetime raised on another planet.

Luci was looking for the correct building to get to her next class when she bumped into a Synnr woman and almost knocked her over. The woman's wings flared out so she could catch her balance, and she pulled them in almost as quickly.

Luci wished she'd kept them out. Zulir wings were so freaking cool and she wanted to study them, but it seemed kind of impolite to ask people to display them when they didn't want to. The woman appeared to be a little bit older than Luci, though most people on the campus were. Synnrs went to college later than humans, as a rule. They tended to get some life experience before pursuing higher education. As a matter of fact, Luci appeared to be one of the youngest people on campus.

Fuck.

She hated being the youngest. She was the youngest among her human friends and the youngest among the students. Was there anyone on this freaking moon she was older than?

"Are you alright?" the Zulir woman asked.

Luci clutched her learning tablet to her chest and nodded, shifting her bag over one shoulder as it threatened to fall. "I'm fine. I'm so sorry." She felt like a klutz and she hated it. She used to be coordinated.

The woman smiled. "It's all right. You look a little lost."

She looked so nice that Luci wanted to give her a big hug and beg her to be friends. But that wasn't something that adults did, so Luci just grimaced. "Is it that obvious? I have to get to math class," she said.

"Me too. My name is Hanna." She gave Luci an inviting smile. Maybe friendships wouldn't be as hard as she feared.

"Luci."

Hanna, it seemed, knew where to go, and she led Luci into the introductory math class they were both enrolled in. They sat beside each other but didn't have much time to talk before the professor, a Synnr man, came in and started lecturing.

The numbers didn't look the same as what Luci was used to back on Earth, but the concepts were. It appeared that math was math no matter where she was in the galaxy. It was the first time in Luci's life that she was relieved to be surrounded by numbers.

They listened to the lecture for about an hour before the professor gave them guidance on what to read before their next class and dismissed them.

Luci followed Hanna out of the class for no other reason than it seemed that the Zulir woman knew where she was going. "That wasn't too bad, was it?"

Hanna asked. "Though I remember what my math scores were like in school. This doesn't bode well."

"I'm afraid that math is going to be my best subject," Luci admitted. "Numbers are numbers, right? That's about the only thing that I feel comfortable with right now."

"How's that?" Hanna asked. She looked vaguely concerned at what Luci was saying, but still polite enough not to pry.

And Luci didn't want her to pry.

There were plenty of people that knew the whole sad story about her life and what had happened, and she didn't want everyone on campus to find out that she was a poor abducted human and victim of the Apsyns. She wanted them to know her as herself. She didn't want pity, and she didn't want to be the object of curious looks. It had to be obvious that she wasn't from Osais. She didn't need to add more fuel to that fire.

"That's just how it is," Luci said and hoped that made sense. She looked around, trying to figure out which building had her next class, when she spotted a group of four soldiers walking across a grassy field. "What's that all about?" They were supposed be safe here. Why were soldiers patrolling the campus?

"Probably just some of the stuff going on with the war. It's nothing to be worried about," Hanna said, so nonchalantly that Luci had to pause a minute to parse what she was saying. How could she be so unconcerned about a *war*?

"I think there's always something to be worried about when it comes to the Apsyns." Luci couldn't keep the fear and disgust out of her voice. The Apsyns had tried to destroy her, and now they were trying to destroy her new home. She wouldn't be happy until this whole thing was over. And maybe not after that, either.

"Why do you think that?" asked Hanna. She leaned closer to Luci and the look on her face was strange—not quite a smile, but like she was trying to fake it.

"It's a long story," and Luci wasn't about to tell it.

Hanna's communicator beeped, and she shot Luci an apologetic smile. "I have another class across campus. It was good to meet you. See you tomorrow." And then she was off.

Luci watched her go and then checked her schedule one more time to see where she was headed. She was going to need to study a campus map if she had any hope of surviving the year.

When she looked back up, Ax was standing right in front of her, and her heart skipped a beat. She hadn't seen him since her birthday party, but that wasn't the entire story. Her cheeks flamed as she thought of that night and all the possibility it entailed. But he wasn't supposed to show up on campus. There were boundaries.

Or there would be. If she put them down.

Had he appeared from nowhere? Could he teleport? He was dressed in a soldier's uniform, but unlike the other soldiers she had seen before, he wasn't standing around with the rest of his unit. Luci almost leaned in and gave him a hug, and she could see that he bent down as if he was about to kiss her, but he pulled back at the last moment.

"Hi," said Luci, feeling like the most awkward person in the universe.

"Hello," responded Ax. Well, at least Luci wasn't alone in awkwardness.

She wasn't sure how she was supposed to act around him after what had happened at her birthday party. They were in public. They hadn't been in public together since... Well. Luci wasn't going to think about that.

She might've been able to think of the proper thing to say if her mind hadn't been all scrambled from thinking about the Apsyns and all of the terror they could inflict on her.

Ax was one of the warriors who had rescued her. And the only one that she had ever kissed.

She probably should have a conversation with him. They *probably* needed to talk. Instead, they just stood staring at each other awkwardly.

Luci couldn't do this. Her heart was beating so fast she was worried it would explode, and her breath stuttered uneasily. This wasn't the physical response she wanted to anyone, especially not a man who showed up in her naughtiest dreams.

So she did the only thing she could and said, "I've got to go to class, I'll see you later." And she fled.

2

Ax: I can't wait until I kiss you again.

One Week Ago

The party was in full swing, but the birthday girl was nowhere to be found. Ax wasn't sure why he was looking for Luci, but he was. He wasn't sure if anyone else had noticed that she was hiding. For most of the night she'd been dancing with friends and demanding the attention that came from being the life of the party. It was her night and she was living it to the fullest.

Or she had been until Jori showed up with his date.

It was no secret that Luci had a crush on Jori. She hadn't been trying to hide it. In fact, Ax was pretty sure that Jori was the only one who was oblivious to it.

Or maybe he wasn't oblivious. Maybe *that* was why he had showed up with a guest on his arm. And why they'd been dancing so close for the past hour.

Whatever the reason, Ax didn't want Luci sulking on her special day.

He told himself he only cared because it was her party. He and Luci hadn't spent any time together, and he couldn't really call them friends. But there was something about her that sent him running into the maze that was Crowze's garden to find her.

He found her hiding down one of the greenery laden paths. She wasn't crying and her face wasn't red, which he took as good signs. They might have been from different planets, but some signs of sadness were universal.

"What are you doing here?" It was an obvious question to ask, but Ax needed to say something. He wasn't too good on his feet, so he just said the first thing that came to mind. No one would ever accuse him of being a genius, but at least he cared.

Luci forced a smile, but her blue eyes remained pained. "I just needed a few minutes to myself." The smile got brittle and then drooped. She shook her head a bit and grimaced.

Ax was no expert on human body language, but he was pretty sure he didn't need to be at the moment. She wasn't happy and she didn't want to perform.

"Oh. Would you like me to leave you alone?" His entire purpose had been to bring her back to the party, but everyone needed a few minutes to themselves every now and then.

"No, it's fine." It didn't sound fine.

They didn't say anything after that for several moments. Ax just stood next to her and breathed in the warm night air. Not that anyone would know it was night without the aid of a timepiece. The sun didn't set on Aorsa during the summer, and it would be months until they experienced a full night again.

"I don't really care that he came here with her," said Luci, shifting on her feet a bit before crossing and then uncrossing her arms.

"Okay." What was Ax supposed to say? If she needed to talk, he had ears.

"I don't. I'm not kidding." She glared, but not directly at him.

"I understand that. I'm agreeing with you." He had to suppress a smile. She'd probably claw at him if he showed even a hint of mirth.

"You're placating me," she shot back, challenge flashing in her eyes. "You think I'm a kid." The glare got stronger and turned on him.

But he didn't. Not at all.

He'd been attracted to her the moment he saw her

with her sharp eyes, golden hair, and strong spirit. He'd been wondering if it would be appropriate to make a move, but given the trauma that she and her friends had gone through, he wasn't sure she was ready for something… sensual.

And while he liked Luci and liked the look of her, he also wasn't ready to jump straight into a relationship. Though he might have been getting ahead of himself.

"You know that I'm not much older than you, right?" He'd been lumped in with Jori, Oz, and the others, but some would call him a babe in arms compared to them.

"You're not?" Luci uncrossed her arms and the glare lessened a bit. But only a bit.

Sometimes Ax resented the way others treated him for his age, but he wanted to make Luci comfortable. "I'm twenty-three. I think by some counts, that makes you ancient compared to me."

That made her laugh. Luci was celebrating her nineteenth birthday, but by some counts she was eighty-nine. She had been abducted from Earth and placed in stasis for seventy years along with all the other humans who were abducted by the Apsyns for nefarious purposes. She hadn't aged or even known about the stasis until a few months before. At first, the humans had been angry that any chance to return home had been ripped from them, but he'd begun to hear them joke about their "true" ages.

"Yeah, if I was back home I could finally buy a beer."

Ax didn't see what beer had to do with anything. "You can buy beer." Why would that even be an issue?

Luci rolled her eyes with an indulgent smile. Something deep inside of him unfurled to see her smile like that. "In the country that I'm from, the age limit is twenty-one."

He sputtered. "That's ridiculous."

"That's what a lot of people my age say."

They shared another laugh, and Ax was happy he'd found Luci. He hadn't known she possessed cutting wit and a smile that made him think of dark winter nights together, but now he had even more to add to his thoughts about her.

Luci took a step towards him. "You really don't think that I'm a kid?" She ran a finger on his arm and Ax had to suppress the shiver.

Ax breathed in deep. Her scent mixed with the plants and flowers all around them. His cock stirred, even more interested now, and he tried to get himself under control. He hadn't followed Luci here to make anything happen. But now she was looking at him with want in her eyes, and he couldn't help but feel the same.

"I don't think that you're a kid." He didn't recognize the growl of his voice, but it was all adult desire.

She leaned in, and Ax had to bend down to kiss her. He was much taller than she was, but once he had his arms around her he didn't care. She yielded to him, her tongue swiping against his and tangling, making him groan. Her skin was soft under his fingers, and he couldn't help but imagine what it would be like to see her blonde hair laid out on his bed.

He combed his fingers through her hair, careful not to pull, but luxuriating in the soft feel of the golden strands.

Maybe Ax should thank Jori for bringing someone else to the party.

Luci made a sound of desire that had Ax's cock perking up to attention. If there was just a bit more privacy, if there was no chance of being caught, he might have asked her for more.

But while they were in an obscured location, anyone could walk by at any minute. Of course, an entire pack of loud animals could have stampeded by and Ax would not have heard them, his whole self given over to the kiss.

Luci was the one to pull back. They were both breathing heavily and her eyes were hooded with want. "Yes," he said.

Luci laughed. "What?"

"To anything you want. Yes to anything." He'd take her away from this place right now if it meant he could have her. He didn't have riches, but at the moment he'd promise her the galaxy for another kiss.

"I don't want anything," she said. Ax couldn't help the rush of disappointment. There was a promise in that kiss, something more than just a moment on her birthday.

He might not have been eager to jump into something before he'd chased after Luci, but it had only taken a few minutes for his mind to change. "So if I were to ask you if you wanted to go out sometime..."

Her face grew serious. "I'm not really looking for a relationship right now."

It should have been what he wanted to hear. He didn't, not after a kiss like that.

"But..." she offered, "if you wanted to do more of *that* without a relationship, I could be convinced."

Ax grinned. Yeah. He could be convinced too.

3

Luci: Thanks.

Ax: For what?

Luci: Knowing I'm not broken.

Ax: Of course you're not.

Luci: Enough of that. If you had one day left to live, who would you do?

Ax: Don't you mean what?

Luci: You know I don't.

LUCI WAS the first one to arrive at Crowze's house for lunch. Or was it Zac's house now? He'd moved in with his Matches not too long ago, leaving one less human living at Human House. The place was beginning to feel a bit lonely as more people Matched.

Okay, that was a bit of an exaggeration.

The table was set up on the patio out back where they looked out over Crowze's manicured gardens and all of the beauty that they contained. It was way nicer than any yard Luci had ever seen. Weird to think that it was hers too, kind of. She and the other humans were living at Human House just down the way, everything provided by Crowze and his vast wealth.

It was what allowed her to go to college. But she hoped one day that she would be able to support herself. She doubted she would ever be able to pay the Synnr warrior back for his generosity, and she didn't think he would accept money even if she tried to offer it, but she couldn't depend on him forever.

Zac came out one of the back doors, his pale cheeks red with a flush. She didn't see either Crowze or Grace, but from the look on Zac's face he must have just been with one or both of them.

Before Luci got a chance to tease him, Emily showed up and took a seat at the table. Her hair was pulled back in a tight bun, and she wore a military style jacket over her street clothes. Borrowed from her mate? Or was that part of the uniform she'd been assigned since joining the Synnr military at Oz's side?

Luci didn't have a chance to ask before the servants brought out their meal.

If she ignored all of the trauma from the alien

abduction, her life really *had* improved since leaving Earth. The closest she'd ever had to a servant was a Roomba.

She turned to make a comment to Emily, but Emily was looking at her communicator with a silly smile on her face. Luci would have bet just about any dollar amount that Oz was the one who had put that smile on Emily's face.

Luci had to suppress a scowl. She didn't want a mate. She didn't need it. She could make a life for herself.

Between Zac's kiss-flushed cheeks and Emily's smile, she hated that she felt a little bit left out. A few of her friends found mates and suddenly she was wondering what it was like.

She wasn't going to think about Ax.

A few kisses didn't make a relationship. And she had flat out told him that she didn't want more than something physical.

She meant it. Really.

She was *pretty* sure.

But that didn't mean that she couldn't feel a bit left behind.

"How was your first day of school?" Zac asked once he settled into his chair.

Back on Earth, Zac had been a scholar, and his knowledge of English literature had gotten him close to the Synnr Queen, who loved hearing the stories that he told. If anyone else was going to try college, Luci guessed it would be Zac. So she knew the question wasn't just idle curiosity.

"It's a culture shock," she had to admit. "I have almost no foundation of knowledge of the things that everyone seems to know. They all make these references that I don't get. And math is my best subject, which is just something that should *never* be true." She shuddered at the thought. Luci had never been a great student, but she'd always been good enough. Still, that didn't mean that math was something that she had ever liked.

A laugh burst out of Zac.

But Emily grimaced. "I was never much of a scholar."

"Yeah, but you can do flips and stuff, it's super awesome." Luci had seen Emily in action, and it had been almost enough to make her forget about the terrible situation they'd been in. Emily had been a competitive gymnast before she was abducted and had spent most of her life dedicated to that. Luci didn't know what it was like to be dedicated to anything to develop it to that level. She had just gone through life doing what was expected of her and doing it all right enough that no one questioned it. She was hoping that college on Aorsa would give her direction. Would help her figure out what she wanted. But she wasn't sure if that was going to happen.

"And what about Ax?" Emily asked.

Luci jolted at the question. "Ax? What about Ax?" Luci's heart rate kicked up at the thought that Emily and Zac had any idea of what was or was not going on between her and Ax.

She and Ax had made out at her birthday party, and since then she had sent a couple exciting texts to his communicator, which he had enthusiastically responded to. But nothing besides that.

It was nothing. It meant nothing.

And she definitely wasn't about to tell Emily or Zac about it.

"You're blushing." Zac was vibrating and grinning in his seat.

"Shut up." Luci winced at her tone. She sounded like a defensive kid, and that was only putting blood in the water for the two sharks who were circling her.

"I thought you were into Jori," Emily said innocently, the little devil. "What's going on with Ax?"

"Jori's so last month." She couldn't hold the denial back.

Why was everyone obsessed with her little crush on Jori? The one that was completely over? Sure, she had liked him for a while. She didn't like him anymore. Ever since the jerk had showed up at her birthday party with another woman.

Was she being defensive? Maybe, but she really, truly, *absolutely* did not have a crush on Jori.

And she was not going to think about whether or not Ax had anything to do with that.

"So how is life in the big house going?" she asked Zac, desperate for something to take the attention off of her.

Zac launched into a monologue about life with Crowze and Grace, full of anecdotes and blushes, and Luci relaxed back into her seat, relieved that the diversionary tactic had worked.

For now.

But apparently she wasn't as subtle about her relationship, or lack thereof, she thought.

How did Zac and Emily even know?

No one had seen them together.

Right?

She almost asked. But the heat was off of her for now, and she wasn't going to summon it back to herself. Not yet.

She would just have to be more subtle. More chill.

She and Ax could be friends with benefits, and no one besides the two of them needed to know about the benefits. That would work. It sounded like a good idea.

Despite the suggestive texts they had sent back

and forth, Ax hadn't made a move to do anything more. Luci was sick of waiting. If she wanted something to happen, she was going to need to seize the moment and do it herself. So she started forming a plan while she, Zac, and Emily ate their lunch.

Ax wasn't going to know what hit him.

JORI SHOT his spark at Ax as if Ax really were an enemy Apsyn, and Ax barely dodged in time.

They were in a training facility doing one on one exercises to sharpen their skills. Ax was supposed to cross the warehouse and recover a communicator from a lockbox. It was Jori's responsibility to stop that from happening.

But Ax was determined. He wasn't going to fail again.

Especially not against Jori.

But he wasn't quick enough between one move and the next, and Jori's spark almost hit him dead center. Ax dropped to the ground and crawled to a position that would give him cover. He couldn't let Jori beat him.

He wasn't going to lose to the man that Luci had a crush on.

Ax wanted to curse as the thought distracted him. He couldn't be thinking about Luci right now, not in a simulated matter of life and death. And he knew it shouldn't matter. Whatever she felt for Jori, she was kissing him. Not that Jori, or anyone else, knew that.

Another spark flashed his way, and Ax sent out a bolt in response.

It was a mistake. Jori must not have been certain of his position, but now he was, and he trained all of his fire on Ax.

Ax cursed. Stupid mistake. Jori had years of experience on him and was one of the most skilled warriors he'd ever met. Even more importantly, he reveled in battle. If there was anyone in the military that could teach Ax a thing or two, it was Jori. If Ax could get his head out of his ass.

Using his spark as a shield, he ran for different cover—a large pipe and a cleverly positioned stack of crates—and was successful. But he still had a staircase to get up, and Jori had the high ground. There was no getting around that reality.

If Ax went at it directly, he was going to fail. Jori wouldn't just let him up the stairs.

It was times like these that Ax really wished that his wings were functional. But that was not how Zulir wings worked. They could break a fall and allow him to glide, but he couldn't launch himself into the air and fly like a bird. He couldn't waste his time thinking about might have beens, so he looked around for something that might give him an advantage.

There were plenty of obstacles and tools around the warehouse, all set up for the use of the warriors training there. Ax didn't have much time to make a plan, but he did what he could, aiming for one of the light bulbs and shooting out with his spark before causing chaos with his power, a precarious pile of metal toppling over. It was the distraction he needed to get towards the stairs.

But he was only three quarters of the way up when Jori caught him.

It didn't matter. Ax was determined to win.

He sent a punishing jolt of spark at Jori which sent him toppling off the platform he was meant to be defending. Jori crashed into something on the ground below and it sounded painful.

Ax didn't waste time checking to see if Jori was okay. For this mission, he couldn't worry about that.

It took several seconds to unlock the lockbox, but soon Ax's fingers wrapped around the communicator and he held it up in victory.

All the lights in the warehouse came on, and the timer stopped at nine minutes and twenty-seven seconds. He'd been given only ten minutes to complete this mission and he'd done it successfully.

Ax couldn't stop the pleased grin that bloomed

across his face. He'd beaten Jori. Finally. Anyone evaluating him would see this as a success.

Jori was shaking off his fall, but he didn't look too upset that Ax had won.

In fact, he clapped a hand on Ax's back. "Well done."

They headed for the locker room to clean up and change and then both found seats in the lounge, where they snacked on energy bars and drank water to make up for the energy depletion that came from using their sparks that much.

"What was distracting you?" Jori asked. "I thought I had you there for a minute." He said it with the kind of affability he always had. Jori was everyone's friend when they weren't on the battlefield.

"Distracting?" Ax wasn't about to talk about Luci. And he didn't want the man to think that he was thinking with his cock rather than his brain.

But Jori could sniff out gossip with barely any clues. "Sounds like you got yourself a girl," he said with a grin.

Ax didn't want to respond, but if he said nothing, Jori would just make something up. "Something like that." He wasn't going to give Jori anything else.

That didn't stop Jori from prying. "Something like that. What's like? A girl? A boy? Neither? Both? This town runs on gossip and I want it." The gossip part was true, definitely. And Jori was happy to share tidbits with whoever would listen.

It startled a laugh out of Ax. "You just want to throw the scent off yourself. They're starting to wonder if you'll ever settle down." The longest relationship that Ax had ever heard of Jori having was two weeks long. The man didn't do permanent. He didn't do serious about anything. "Do you even want to Match?"

Jori shuddered. "Not if I can help it." His normal affability slipped from his face for a moment before his expression recovered like nothing had happened.

Ax wanted to ask him why. He didn't really get it.

Sure, Ax wasn't exactly ready to settle down in the moment, but in the abstract, some day, he wanted a Match and all that it brought with it. That was part of Zulir life.

How could Jori not want that?

But it wasn't Ax's business. And if he asked Jori he might learn more than he wanted to know.

They wrapped up eventually and Ax headed home. He feared if he stayed with Jori any longer he'd ended up spilling all his secrets, what few he had, without meaning to. And Jori would somehow not give anything in return. It was better to retreat than risk it.

He had barely settled in at his apartment when there was a knock at his door. He wasn't expecting anybody, and he wondered if it was Jori for some reason.

It wasn't.

Ax stared at the security feed for several moments trying to make sense of what he was seeing.

Luci was standing on his doorstep, waiting to be let in.

4

Luci: What are you wearing?

Ax: Why?

Luci: Never mind, it's an Earth thing.

NERVES OR EXCITEMENT?

Luci was shaking with one of them, but she couldn't tell which.

She stood in front of Ax's door and breathed deep, trying to get her heart rate under control. She was here for a reason. She could do this. She wanted him, and she was ready to make this happen.

So why was he taking so long to answer the door?

She had thought of texting him after her lunch with the others, but if she texted him, he could say no. He could still say no with her right on his doorstep, but what guy would? Ugh, Luci knew she was probably going about this all wrong. But her entire life was up in the air, and she wanted to grab something solely for herself.

She wanted Ax.

She remembered just how passionately he had kissed her. He wanted this just as much as she did, if the messages he was sending were anything to go by.

She was just showing a little initiative.

The lock on the door disengaged and it slid open. Ax stood framed in the door wearing a pair of loose fitting pants that hung low on his hips and a dark shirt that was tight enough to show all the stretch of muscle under the fabric.

Her indecision was gone. This was a great choice. But he needed to take that shirt off. She'd spent days imagining what he looked like naked, and it was time to see if her imagination lived up to reality.

"Luci. Hi." He sounded surprised, and why wouldn't he?

Talking was only going to make this awkward.

Luci wasn't here for conversation.

She stepped forward, placing one hand on his chest and feeling those strong muscles of his, and got up on her tiptoes so she could loop her other hand around his head and tug his head down into a searing kiss.

He could pull away. There was no way she could force him to do anything he didn't want to do. But given the surrendering groan that tore out of him, Ax wasn't about to pull back.

He wrapped an arm around her and pulled her fully into his apartment. Distantly, she heard the door slide closed behind them and she had half a thought that one of them should make sure that the lock was engaged, but then Ax's tongue met hers and she forgot to care about privacy.

He hitched her up and she wrapped her legs around him, groaning as she felt his thickening cock between them.

Yup. Best decision ever.

Ax stumbled through the house, as if he was trying to find the perfect place for this make out session. If Luci could have pulled herself away from him, she might have suggested his bed, but she didn't want to stop kissing him long enough to say anything.

After a bit of scrambling, she ended up perched on what she assumed was his kitchen counter, though she wasn't taking much time to memorize what his apartment looked like. It felt like a kitchen counter, and that was good enough for her.

She ran both of her hands through his hair and loved the feel of the soft strands. Ax had a bit of a curl that he usually tamed with some kind of product, but he must have just taken a shower or something because it was a tousled mass of curlicues that made him look a little bit younger than he normally did.

She loved it. They could be young together.

But even better than his hair was his chest. After taking in all the feel of his hair, she tugged at his shirt and separated from him just long enough to pull it over his head and throw it somewhere across the room. She heard something clatter to the floor, but she could care less about what it was.

Ax was kissing her and that was all that mattered.

There was a bit of iridescence to Zulir skin, something that made it different than a human's, and in the right light it looked like the fanciest sci-fi makeup that she could imagine. Luci wanted to find a sketchbook and colored pencils and attempt to draw Ax, even if she had never had a very great talent for sketching. She would learn just so she could dedicate paper to his body.

But if she could not do him justice with her fingers, she would do him justice with her lips. She kissed along his collarbone and his neck, sucking on the skin so she was sure to leave a mark. She had to tell herself this wasn't anything more than casual. That was the whole point of the thing. It didn't matter how good this felt. It was just physical.

Luci tugged her own top off and threw it in the

same direction that she had thrown Ax's shirt. They needed to move this thing along before she started thinking stupid thoughts about wanting a boyfriend or wanting to make this more than it was.

Ax groaned when he saw her breasts and all of the pale skin of her chest and stomach.

"You like?" she asked with a grin. For some reason she had never been particularly modest when it came to her body. Her first boyfriend back in high school had had a problem with that. Her second boyfriend had loved it. Luci liked how she looked. And she liked sharing herself with people who could appreciate it.

Not a lot of people. Just the two back on Earth.

And now, just Ax.

He sucked in a ragged breath and surprised her by scooping her back up and moving to a different part of the apartment, where he could set her down on a sofa.

"I like a lot," he said, his voice gone gravelly and eyes dark.

Luci couldn't help the grin. She made Ax look like that, she made him *need*. "Then show me." She wanted to see what he could do.

His lips found her breasts, and Luci bit her lip to keep from making the kind of sound that would embarrass her. She was supposed to be the confident seductress right now, not a girl trading on what was realistically not that much experience. Ax was into it. She was into it. And she didn't want him asking questions at this point.

They were here to make each other feel good. That was all that mattered. And when Ax kissed down her stomach and to the buckle of her pants, she couldn't stop shivering.

"You like?" He rolled his eyes up at her with a grin.

"I like," she said, embarrassed at how breathy it came out. "Keep going."

AX WAS BLESSED by the gods, and he wasn't going to overthink whatever was going on between him and Luci.

Luci had shown up on his doorstep powered by some sort of sensual spirit, and she had him by the cock before he could think to offer her even the most basic hospitality.

Her skin was soft under his lips and fingers, and she tasted so sweet. He needed to memorize the flavor and scent of her, because he wasn't sure if this was ever going to happen again.

He could sense a bit of desperation in her, and he

didn't know if it was powered by whatever had sent her to him or by pure lust.

He was hoping it was lust.

Because the longer this went on, the more he was a slave to it.

He carefully pulled her pants down until she was naked before him and splayed out on his couch. She looked like she belonged there, her pale hair and skin contrasted against the dark brown material of the sofa. She would look even better in his bed.

But he couldn't bring her there. Luci said she didn't want feelings involved. She wanted this to be casual. And if he got her in his bed he didn't think he would ever let her leave.

Ax's cock jerked at the thought, and he reached down to readjust himself before it fully took control.

He would give her everything she wanted and more, and then he would put his whole self into making it so she wanted to be in his bed to stay there for good.

But right now he just wanted her wrung out with pleasure.

And that was what his tongue was for.

He kissed up one leg until he made it to the heat of her core, where he delved in without hesitation. Luci's gasp had him feeling like a god, and the way she squirmed and begged for more told him that he was doing exactly the right thing.

Her scent and taste surrounded him, and Ax never wanted to leave this spot as he worshipped her like the sexual goddess she was.

He held her anchored in place and grinned against her sex when one of her hands stroked through his hair to keep him where he was, a silent command to keep going.

Nothing could have stopped him. Nothing except a word from her.

And when she bucked against him, gasping out his name and saying she was close, he didn't stop. Not until she was whimpering and crying, her flesh rippling around him.

He finally pulled back and looked up at her to see her eyes a little dazed and sex drunk, a broad grin spread across panting lips. "Good job. A plus. Gold star."

He understood some of those words. But sometimes the translator that was allowing them to communicate was a little too literal. Ax was *almost* certain he got the gist of what she was saying.

His cock was so hard that it hurt, and he wanted to sink himself deep into the depths of her tight heat, but something made him hold back. This was only their second encounter. And he wanted more than just this. A wiser man might have pressed his advantage at this moment, but now that Ax had Luci spread out and sated before him, he was determined to make this something that could last.

"Come here," Luci said, beckoning him forward with a limp hand. "And take off your pants."

Ax didn't need to be told twice. He shucked off his pants and joined her on the sofa, even if he wasn't going to fuck her right now.

But that wasn't what Luci had in mind. She wrapped her fingers around his cock and stroked. "This good?" she asked with a happy little grin, as if she was fascinated by the feel of him.

The sound that Ax made wasn't rightly defined as a word, but she understood exactly what he meant.

Yes. A plus. Gold star.

She stroked him, and he thrust into her fist until his vision whited out, his cock started to vibrate, and he came.

Luci was all smiles and she kissed him again.

He settled in beside her and pulled her close. His body was sated, and that should have been satisfaction enough, but he wanted more. Needed more.

"I should probably get going," Luci said, but she didn't sound completely enthusiastic about hunting for her clothes and taking off.

"Stay a while," he asked.

She didn't say yes, but she snuggled back into him, and pretty soon the action of the day and the activities of the night piled up and he slipped into unconsciousness, with Luci bundled up tight beside him.

He didn't know how long he slept, but when he rose from his nap, Luci was gone.

5

Luci: Sometimes I have nightmares that I'm back on Kilrym.

Luci: Ugh. Ignore that. Sorry to bother you.

Ax: You're not bothering me. I want to make you feel safe.

LUCI LOOKED at the message on her communicator with a smile.

I wish you had stayed the night.

Ax had sent it the morning after their encounter two days ago. At first she had been proud of herself for waking up in time to walk out. It was a sign she wasn't getting too close.

Staying the night felt too intimate. She was there for a reason. She got off, Ax got off, what more was there to want?

But he wished that she had stayed the night.

It was validation that he wanted her. And maybe validation that they were getting too close.

It felt crazy to even think it.

They'd kissed more than they had talked. But Luci had to wonder if she was doing the right thing. She could feel emotions threatening her equilibrium, and she didn't want to get in too deep. Ax was as nice as they came. And the way he had kissed her, had touched her, it went deeper than just the physical.

She wished she had stayed the night too. But she wasn't going to stay the night, and she wasn't going to get too attached.

She was going to get off and that was it.

Luci nodded to herself and hoped she didn't look weird to anyone on the campus around her. She was too young to get attached. She had to figure out who she was and what she was doing with the rest of her life by herself. Her decision was made and she was happy about it.

And then Ax crossed her path and her heart flipped.

Damn it. She was trying to be all adult and shit. Her heart was *not* the organ that was supposed to be getting involved with this.

Ax smiled at her, and she couldn't help but smile back and give him a little wave. That was fine. There was also the friends part that came with friends with benefits, and smiling and nodding and maybe talking a little bit had to be expected. It didn't mean she was falling in love with the guy or anything.

Love? No. Not a bit.

She wasn't a kid. She wasn't going to fall for the first guy who gave her an orgasm. Besides, he wasn't even the first guy to have given her an orgasm so that didn't count.

Luci squeezed her eyes shut and gave her head another shake. She really needed to stop thinking about Ax and orgasms at all. They could hook up later and do whatever, but she wasn't going to think about him today.

Of course, when she opened her eyes, he wasn't looking at her anymore. Instead, he was smiling at a Synnr woman and pointing her in the direction of another building on the campus. A flash of something like jealousy scorched through Luci, and she spun around so she wasn't forced to look at him. She had no claim on him. And he was just doing his job. And it wouldn't matter if that wasn't the case.

He wasn't her boyfriend. He could talk to whoever he wanted.

And, she supposed, if he was her boyfriend, he could still talk to whoever he wanted because she didn't own him or anything like that.

Luci sank to the ground with a groan and put her

bag down beside her. She had a while before her class and she was in a nice green space that seemed like a good place to relax.

She wasn't the only one who had that idea. Plenty of other students were milling around, some like her sitting down on the grass, others laying, and a few throwing a ball back and forth. It could have been a normal Earth university, or it might have been until she saw those people playing catch start to use their sparks to send the ball every which way.

Yeah, she wasn't on Earth anymore. Luci closed her eyes for a moment to better soak up the sun. She kind of loved the twenty-two hours—the length of an Aorsan day—of sunlight. She didn't know what she was going to do in the winter. But she would deal with that when it came.

"Shouldn't we be getting to class?" a familiar voice asked from beside her.

Luci turned her head and then angled upward to see Hanna standing beside her, her books clutched to her chest. She looked a bit frazzled, as if she had been rushing to and fro, and Luci wondered what kind of class she had before their math class that had her running all over the place.

Luci didn't think she had actually fallen asleep so she checked her watch. "We still have thirty minutes before class," she said. "It's too nice out to go inside yet." She patted the ground beside her, an invitation for Hanna to sit.

Hanna sat for a moment, but she didn't look relaxed. She kept looking at her watch and then looking at the math building. "I'm kind of thirsty. Do you want to get something to drink before class. Keep our minds sharp?"

Luci reached into her own bag and held up an energy drink that she had brought with her. "I'm good, thanks."

"Oh." Hanna fidgeted and then looked back and forth again. "Are you sure? They have really good snacks at the café too."

Luci had to laugh. If she headed to the café, she worried she wouldn't go to class at all. Math might currently be her best subject, but that didn't mean she liked it. "I'm not hungry. I just ate breakfast before heading to campus."

She didn't know what Hanna's issue was. Maybe she should have been polite and gone with her to get a drink or something, but Luci was comfortable and she didn't want to move.

Hanna finally heaved a sigh and stood up. "I guess I'll see you in class," she said. Then she took off, probably to go get that drink she was talking about.

Luci watched her walk away and wondered if she should get up and chase after her. It only occurred to her after Hanna left that she might have been making overtures of friendship.

Friends inconvenienced themselves sometimes, getting up from casual sunbathing to go to a café to get a drink. Maybe Luci should have done that.

She was trying to make this life for herself, and she was still messing things up.

But Hanna was already gone, and Luci wasn't completely sure where she was headed. There were a couple cafés, and if Luci guessed wrong she would be spending all of the rest of her break time chasing Hanna down.

She would see her in math class, and then she would see if they wanted to meet for a snack before their next class. That was the grown-up thing to do.

Luci was going to rock adulthood.

Then she flinched. She was pretty sure adults didn't think things like that.

She was an adult. She would fight anyone who said she wasn't. Hell, she was technically older than most of the people on this campus. But she was still just nineteen and trying to figure this stuff out.

Luci let her eyes fall closed again while the sun soaked into her skin. One of the nicest things to learn about the sun in the system was that it wasn't strong enough to leave a sunburn on human skin. Emily had been the first one to realize that, and since Luci was just as pale as Emily, she reaped the benefits just as much. She could fall asleep and doze for hours without waking up to red blisters and pain.

But she only had about twenty more minutes. Luci thought that maybe she should set a timer just so she didn't accidentally end up late for class, but she drifted off before she could do it.

She heard the sounds of her fellow students, but eventually they faded as she slipped into sleep.

She woke to the sound of screams.

CHAOS ERUPTED around them between one breath and the next.

Ax had heard people say that they could sense when something bad was coming, but this wasn't like that. The day had been as nice as any, and he thought it would be just another boring stretch of hours spent at the University of Aorsa.

He was wrong.

So wrong.

Smoke rolled out of the windows and doors of a nearby building and a handful of students rushed out, their wings wrapped around them in defense while they screamed.

About five made it out before the doors slammed shut.

"It's Apsyns," said his partner. "They're taking the Red Building."

The Red Building was the science building where most of the labs and science classes were held. It was four stories tall and could have held hundreds of people. Ax didn't know exactly how many there were right now, and that chaos was bound to get people killed.

"Do we have anybody inside?" he asked his partner, Felyx.

Felyx shook his head.

They both had blasters, but they left those in their holsters as they unfurled their wings and readied their sparks.

Ax knew that Luci was outside somewhere. He had seen her earlier, though she had disappeared from his vision almost as quickly. He wanted to plunge into the mass of students running and screaming and see if he could find her. He needed her to be safe.

But the Red Building was his priority. That was where the enemy was.

He only hoped that they didn't come outside looking for more trouble.

A student wearing a t-shirt of a popular Synnr sports team ran past him and Ax grabbed her arm to stop her.

"What's going on?" she asked, voice laced with fear.

"Round up the students and get them to the Green Building," he told her. Someone needed to do crowd control, and they didn't have enough Synnr soldiers on the campus to do it. Reinforcements would come, but they would get here too late.

The Synnr girl didn't look too enthused at the prospect, but she quickly got the attention of one student and then another and another before taking them across the quad to the Green Building, where most of the history classes were held.

Ax hoped those were the correct instructions. He hoped whatever chaos the Apsyns were trying to cause didn't spread to other buildings.

He and Felyx headed for the Red Building. They didn't know how many enemies were inside, nor how many potential hostages. But they would figure that out in the process.

"I messaged headquarters," Felyx said before they entered the building. "We've got more soldiers coming." But they both knew it would take time for reinforcements to arrive.

They could wait outside for the half an hour or so that it would take for more people to show up to help them, but if they waited that long, Ax knew that people would die. They had to hope that they could stop this before things got out of hand.

As if things weren't out of hand already.

"Let's go." Ax hoped that Synnr girl found Luci and got her into the Green Building. He gave it one last thought before he forced worries about Luci out of his mind. If he worried about her, he'd get himself killed. And if he was dead, there was no way to protect her.

If he had thought that the outside was chaotic, inside the building was even worse. A blast of his spark was enough to get them past the doors.

It appeared that whatever had caused them to close and lock was only the normal building security system, not some special treat left for them to counteract by the Apsyns.

A handful of students and a teacher or two rushed out of the doors as soon as Ax's spark blasted them off their hinges. But once those people were out, Ax and Felyx were left alone in a long, narrow hallway completely devoid of people.

Papers and bags were scattered on the floor, dropped wherever their owners had cast them aside.

The first floor seemed empty. They headed up the stairs.

It wasn't difficult to find the Apsyns.

There were four of them. One stood outside the doorway to a lab and Felyx managed to take him out with a targeted blast of his spark.

That was the last easy moment of the fight.

Ax went through the door first and one of the Apsyns hit him in the shoulder, sending him flying backwards, where he banged his head against the wall and fell to the floor. But he couldn't stay out for long, not when Felyx was depending on him.

He had no idea what the Apsyns were doing here. This was a college science lab; there were no state secrets or anything important.

What was the point?

But that would be for investigators to decide.

Ax mustered his spark and sent it flying at the nearest Apsyn.

Felyx was clearly a better fighter, able to send out targeted jolts with the kind of precision that Ax could only dream of.

The Apsyns got their own hits in, but they clearly hadn't expected to be met with resistance so quickly.

The fight didn't last that long.

Ax took out one of the Apsyns, while Felyx took out the other two, leaving all four in an unconscious heap on the floor.

Ax hadn't managed to stand back up before the fight was over.

Felyx gave him a helping hand up, and Ax winced from the damage his body had taken.

"This was barely a fight. Does it always hurt this much?" Ax groaned and rubbed his hip, trying to make the pain go away.

Felyx laughed, his eyes bright with energy. "Hurt? I feel great."

Ax crossed the lab to the window and looked out on the quad to see what was going on down there. The students had mostly cleared out, and he didn't see any other Apsyns causing trouble.

Good.

Even better, he saw an official Synnr military vehicle drive up to the entrance of the Red Building. Four Synnr soldiers piled out and his communicator crackled with the confirmation of their arrival.

Things happened quickly after that. The Apsyns were taken into custody, Ax's wounds were tended to by a medic, and he and Felyx were commanded to report to headquarters in the morning.

The day was almost over by the time he and Felyx were dismissed. But still Ax took a few minutes to look around for Luci. He would have sent a message, but he been commanded to only use his communicator for official business while on the campus. He wasn't about to disobey an order like that.

The students had been evacuated from the Green Building and sent home. The campus would close for a day, but was planning to reopen once they had secured it.

Luci wasn't there. He could contact her when he got home.

Or maybe he should head over to her place to make sure she was doing okay.

No. He didn't think she would like that.

Though he wasn't sure.

Ax sat in his vehicle for several minutes arguing with himself about whether or not he should go to Crowze's estate, where the humans all lived.

He decided against it. Barely. He figured he could always change his mind.

And he was dealing with second thoughts the entire drive back to his place.

But as soon as he walked up the steps to his apartment, he knew he had made the right choice.

Luci was sitting right in front of his door.

6

———

Ax: You like? (Attached: an image of glistening abs)

Luci: I'd like it better if you were here and I could lick them myself.

Luci had to see if Ax was okay.

That was her main thought as she rushed from the campus to his apartment. It wasn't a surprise to find that he wasn't home. Of course he wasn't. He had responsibilities. But she sat herself in front of his door and waited. Maybe she should have sent him a text.

Maybe that would have been enough.

But Luci couldn't make herself get up and go home, not matter how uncomfortable the hard ground was under her butt. She waited for hours, anxiety churning in her guts at the thought of what might have happened to Ax. She'd only seen him for a moment as he and his partner stormed into the Red Building to deal with whatever trouble the Apsyns were causing.

He'd looked like a real hero.

She wished he was a coward.

She would never tell him that. There was no way he would take it the right way. But she didn't want him to get hurt.

It was too bad that he was a soldier and was pretty much destined for injury.

She heard footsteps coming up the stairs and turned to look toward the entryway. A few people had already come and gone, and she expected this would be the same, but this time it was Ax, right there in the flesh.

He looked tired. There were bags under his eyes and his uniform was wrinkled, something she hadn't thought was possible. The sharp angles of his face were even sharper than usual, as if he had lost weight in the hours since she had last seen him.

Maybe using his spark took a toll like that.

But he was here.

He was safe.

Ax looked at her for several moments, and in that time, Luci managed to get to her feet. She didn't know what she wanted to say. She kept telling herself that the thing between them was only physical, but if that was true she wouldn't have been here. She wouldn't have cared.

The words still wouldn't come, so she closed the distance between them and wrapped her arms around him. She wanted to hug him tight, but Ax winced, so she loosened her grip.

An injury? Bruises? He was walking, so that was good. But she was sure there was something wrong.

"Would you like to come inside?" Ax asked, his lips brushing against her hair in what she could fool herself into thinking was a caring caress.

"Yes." She'd come all this way. Even if she was still a bit confused on what she was feeling right now, she definitely wanted inside. She still couldn't quite convince herself that this wasn't a dream. She needed to take more time to see that Ax was truly okay.

He led her inside and went straight to his kitchen, where he pulled two bottles of something from his refrigerator. He offered one to Luci and she took it gratefully, taking a sip and savoring the sweetness. Ax took his own drink, tipping his head back and gulping the liquid down. She couldn't help but stare at the way his throat moved as it swallowed.

He put the half empty bottle down on his counter and looked at her. "How are you doing? The attack must have taken a toll."

Luci didn't want to think about herself right now.

She had made it this far by ignoring anything that could fuck up her emotions.

"Are you okay?" she asked. She didn't like the way he'd winced when she hugged him, and she would fight any Apsyn who did him physical harm. No one got to hurt Ax.

He shrugged and took another gulp of his drink. "I was hit, but I'm fine. A medic took a look on campus."

Hit. What was that supposed to mean? Luci had seen the damage that a direct hit from someone's spark could do. It was like being struck by lightning. Sure, it seemed like Zulir bodies absorbed the damage better than humans would, but that didn't mean that it didn't hurt.

"Hit? What kind of hit? Are you hurt?" She was far enough away from him that she couldn't tear off his shirt to look for the offending wound, but she had to root herself in place to keep from crossing the room to check out the damage.

And Ax could see just how much it was bothering her. He put his drink down again and beckoned her towards his bathroom, pulling his shirt off in the process.

At another time, Luci would have taken the opportunity to ogle his muscles. And they were nice. They were always nice. But her eyes were drawn to the large white bandage that covered up half of his side. It wasn't bloody or anything like that, but its existence offended her.

Ax had a bench in his bathroom, and he sat on it after pulling out a small first aid kit and setting it by his side. "The medic said I should change the bandage and apply some more healing cream when I got home," he said. "Would you like to help?"

She knew he could do it himself. The Apsyns had been kind enough to wound him in a conveniently reachable place. But she was here, and getting her hands on him was the only way she was going to convince herself that he really was okay.

Luci washed her hands quickly and knelt in front of him. She peeled off the bandage as carefully as she could and winced in sympathy as it pulled on some of Ax's chest hair.

"Sorry." The apology slipped out.

"It's not your fault," he assured her.

She knew that. That wasn't why she was apologizing.

He had a tub of something called healing cream and some more bandages available in the first aid kit. But first Luci looked at the wound. It didn't look like much. It was already scabbing over and covered in an oily substance that might have been whatever the medic coated it with. It was like Neosporin on steroids. But it still looked like it hurt. And it must have been worse even an hour ago.

She wanted to hunt down every Apsyn she could find and make them pay for hurting Ax.

But she had him in front of her now, and she had to help him in any way she could.

She dipped her fingers into the container of healing cream and rubbed it over the wound as gently, but thoroughly as she could. Ax winced again, and she had to make herself keep going. His wound needed the care, and sometimes a little bit of tough love was necessary.

It only took a minute or two for her to get the wound completely covered, and then she reapplied the bandage and went to wash her hands again. As she was drying them off, they started to shake. She clenched them on the basin and breathed deep, trying to steady herself.

Ax was right there. He was okay. She had done her bit to help.

So why did she feel like this?

She raised her hands from the base, but they were still shaking. She couldn't turn around and look at Ax. He was the one who was hurt. He was the one who should be dealing with things. Why was she the one freaking out? She wasn't hurt. She was completely fine. She had gotten to safety before much of anything had happened.

But her body didn't seem to realize that.

She felt the air move around her and realized Ax

had come to stand by her. He placed a hand on her shoulder, and she spun around and buried her face against his naked chest. She shouldn't have enjoyed how good he smelled, but she couldn't help it when her nose was right against his skin.

Ax held her close, and eventually Luci's shaking stopped.

She looked up and met his eyes and saw the question right there. She gave him a nod.

He leaned down and kissed her.

AX LED Luci out of the bathroom and sat down beside her on his couch. He kissed her again, as gently as he could manage with the desperate need to touch her roaring through him. She'd come to care for him when he needed it most. He'd wanted to see her so much, but he never would have dreamed she would feel the same.

He knew he shouldn't let his heart get involved. He knew what Luci said she wanted. But he was already in too deep.

Every moment her fingers had pressed against him applying the healing cream had been its own sweet torture. He could have done it himself. He probably *should* have done it himself. But he could not resist anything that Luci would give him.

His cock ached with want, and he wanted to take this further.

But not after the way he had seen his Luci shake.

"You're okay, you're okay, you're okay," Luci kept saying between kisses.

Ax had to choke back a groan as her hand reached down, careful to avoid his wounded side, and teased his cock through his pants. This could turn sensual in a moment.

Who was he kidding? This was already sensual. He could take her to bed and sate their bodies and be done with it. But something made Ax hold back. It wasn't what Luci needed right now. It wasn't what he needed right now. Getting lost in another's body wouldn't heal the hurt that lived in both of them. Not more than temporarily.

So he forced himself to pull back and then cuddled close to Luci, letting her tuck into his side.

This was good. He couldn't say it was better, but different. Comforting.

Perfect in its own imperfect way.

"I didn't want you to get hurt," he said as his mind flashed back to the chaos on campus. "It was all I could think about while I ran into that building." Maybe he shouldn't have confessed that to her. But it wasn't like she would tell his superiors. And the job had been done. They couldn't discipline him for his emotions.

"Me?" She jolted at the confession. "You shouldn't be thinking about me. Not when you're fighting them. I don't want you to get hurt." She clutched an arm around him and squeezed him for emphasis as she gave him those instructions.

The desperate need for closeness took him over and he kissed her again. How could he stop himself? But before the kiss could get too heated he pulled back again. They needed comfort they couldn't find in sex.

"It's so stupid," Luci said. "For a minute back there, all I could think about was when the Apsyns were holding me captive. It was nothing like that. We were never outside on Kilrym, or rarely, I guess. I didn't even see them. But I knew they were there. And all I could think about was being shoved back into a cage for them to do all that stuff to us." She shuddered, and it was Ax's turn to hold her close.

"It's not stupid. I won't let them take you again. They won't get you this time." He didn't know everything that had been done to her, but he had a good idea. Ax would do everything in his power and more to make sure she was safe.

Luci didn't believe him. "You can't promise that."

"Try and stop me." It wasn't the kind of vow that a casual friend would make to another, but Ax didn't care. He meant every word he said, and there was no taking it back.

Luci took several deep breaths, processing what he was telling her. He was afraid that she might deny his vow, push him away. Or push this encounter into something more familiar and easy for the both of them.

But she didn't.

"This isn't what I expected from the college experience," she admitted with a wry smile. She laid her head against his shoulder and let out a sigh, her body relaxing.

Ax played with a strand of her hair and enjoyed the feel of her pressed against him. "What did you expect?" He didn't know what college was like back on Earth. And he had gone to the Military Academy, which was a much different environment than the University of Aorsa.

"Ultimate Frisbee. The scent of pot everywhere. Batting cute guys off with a stick." She grinned up at him at the last one and kissed his cheek.

Maybe he should have felt a flash of jealousy at that, but he could tell she was joking, and he was just glad that she wasn't trying to push him away. "What's Ultimate Frisbee?" He didn't know if her translator was working correctly when it said those words.

She laughed. "I'm not actually sure. But I've heard that it's something that college students do. Frisbees are like these plastic disc things that we throw at one another. I guess they make it a fancy game."

That was no answer to his question. But the talk of strange Earth games led him to share some of the more obscure games he had played with his cousins as a child. And one avenue of conversation led to another, and then another, and another as the hours ticked by and night encroached on them.

Luci yawned and blinked her eyes several times, fighting off sleep.

"I don't want to go home yet," she said. She didn't look at him while she confessed it, but Ax felt it deep in his soul.

"Then stay." He would never send her away. Not when she was everything he wanted.

"All the way till morning," she promised.

Good.

7

---

*Luci: **Thanks** for letting me stay over. I think I would have gone crazy if I had to go home.*

Luci walked down the stairs outside the front of Human House on light feet. She looked over her shoulder and didn't see anyone following her.

Good. Hopefully she could get to class without any more blowups.

"Are you sneaking out?" Gayle Casey asked, coming from around the side of the house.

Luci groaned. Dammit. So close. "No, I'm not." Yeah, that definitely sounded good. No one here could control her comings and goings. No one had that right. So why did she feel like she was breaking curfew?

"That's not cool, Luci," Gayle said as she leaned

against the stone banister at the foot of the steps. "We were worried. We *are* allowed to be worried."

Luci wouldn't consider Gayle a close friend, but the ex-boxer had the potential to become one, if Luci didn't screw it up. But that didn't mean she was going to let the woman act like she was her mother. "I didn't do anything wrong."

Gayle's eyes bugged out. "There was a terrorist attack. You couldn't have sent a note to someone? And you're being all weird about where you ended up. Why?" She was looking at Luci like Luci was her opponent in the ring. No wonder the woman had won so many fights.

Because Ax was hers and she didn't want to talk about it. But if she said that, then she would have to talk about it. "I was somewhere safe. I just needed some time to get my thoughts together. And if I don't take off now, I'm going to be late to class, so we can continue this fight later."

"This isn't a fight."

"Well it sure isn't..." Luci trailed off, unsure of how to end that sentence.

Gayle took mercy on her and shifted the subject. "Are you sure you're ready to go back to school? It's only been two days."

Luci was a little surprised herself that the campus was opened again so quickly, but apparently that was the Synnr way. Not much property had been destroyed, according to reports, and they were beefing up security. They wanted to put on a brave face, so all the students were returning. And Luci would probably be among them.

"I'll be fine." And if she wasn't, well, she would figure it out.

Luckily nothing interesting happened on the way to campus, and Luci was sitting in her seat before math class with plenty of time to spare. She tried not to think about why the Red Building was all locked up, and she didn't waste any time lounging outside. She didn't want to risk a repeat.

Maybe the attack had gotten to her a little bit.

Hanna dropped into the seat right next to her. "I'm glad you're okay," she said. "I didn't have your contact information to check in with you after everything." Hanna's wings were out and glittering in the light. Luci tried not to be jealous.

That made Luci feel a little bit bad. Honestly, she hadn't really thought about Hanna after the attack. Was she a terrible person? Though, to be fair to her, she had known that Hanna was going to the other side of campus before everything happened. So of the two of them, Hanna would have been safer.

"I'm fine, everyone keeps asking, but I'm fine. I promise." Really, Luci just needed this math class to start. God, college was changing her, and not in good ways.

Hanna sighed and slouched back in her chair. "You would've been completely fine if you had just left the quad with me."

"Are you blaming me for being near a terrorist attack?" Though was 'terrorist attack' even the right phrase? There was an actual war going on. Maybe it was just a regular attack. Luci had to stop getting sidetracked. She couldn't believe what Hanna was suggesting.

"Of course I'm not saying that." But there was an unsaid suggestion that it was exactly what she was saying.

"There's no way we could have known something was about to happen. You're not psychic, are you?" The Synnrs had wings and electricity powers; Luci had never heard of any of them having psychic powers. But that would be cool.

"That's not what I meant. I just… You just should have gone with me." Hanna had an intense look on her face, and Luci figured she was dealing with the trauma of the attack in her own way.

"Did you know something was going to happen?" Maybe she wasn't psychic, but perhaps she had seen something. Luci didn't know exactly why she was asking, but she didn't know why Hanna was acting so weird. Something had to be going on.

"Are you suggesting that I'm… That I… Do you think I would *hurt* people?" Hanna glared at her for a moment before scooping up her things and standing up. "That is so wrong. I thought we were friends." She stalked off towards another part of the classroom and sat down by herself.

Luci was confused. What had she said? She hadn't been suggesting that Hanna knew an attack was coming, not really. Not even if she actually asked that. Of course Hanna wouldn't know that.

But she had been really insistent about getting Luci away from the quad.

Had Hanna had some idea that Apsyn assholes were going to strike?

The Apsyns had to get their information from somewhere.

No. That was her brain being stupid and trying to suggest that the one new friend that she made was somehow connected to the Apsyns. That couldn't be true.

Luci would know.

Right?

There wasn't anything physically different between Apsyns and Synnrs, as they were all Zulir. Politically, they were galaxies apart. So if Hanna was an Apsyn, Luci wouldn't be able to tell, at least not by any part of her looks.

But an Apsyn would never intentionally befriend a human. They hated humans. Thought they were not people. They bought them from slavers and performed terrible experiments on them.

There was no reason one of them would be at the University of Aorsa taking a math class.

No *legitimate* reason, anyway.

What was Luci thinking?

Her communicator buzzed and she pulled it out of her pocket, thankful for the distraction. It was from Ax.

The campus is going to be safe today, I promise. No Apsyn is getting past me. Take all the classes you want.

She smiled at the message. Of course Ax couldn't stop every Apsyn, but knowing that he was there did reassure her a little bit.

Something possessed Luci to message back, **Do you want to meet me at the café around lunch time?** It wasn't a date. They were friends. Friends could eat lunch together.

That sounded a little weak even to herself. But it was true. The tone of her messages to and from Ax had changed after the attack. All of yesterday they had messaged back and forth when he wasn't busy with work, and only about half of it had been sexual in nature. They were starting to work on the friends part of their relationship, and she liked that.

But Ax didn't message back before the teacher

came in to start the lesson and she had put her communicator away.

Well, hopefully she would see him later. One way or another.

AX DIDN'T HAVE much time to over analyze the message that Luci sent him. He wanted lunch, of course. But how did she mean it? As a date? As friends? As an assurance that she wasn't going to be assaulted by Apsyns? Any one of them was possible.

He knew she didn't want a relationship, and he had to accept that rather than read into every possible excuse for something more. It didn't matter how much his cock wanted otherwise.

No, his cock was fine, it was his heart that was getting involved.

He was bad at this casual thing. But it wasn't going to make him walk away from Luci.

But he had to get his mind on his job if he was going to keep her safe. He and Felyx were briefing before they started their shift patrolling the campus. They both had thick folders full of intelligence about what had gone wrong and how they could stop it.

Felyx flicked to the first page and read for a while, making interested noises. "Seems like they think the

Apsyns might have been after some research going on in the Red Building."

"Makes sense." It wasn't like the university had top-secret weapons or anything like that, but all universities performed research of one form or another, and maybe the Apsyns knew about a special project.

"And Intel seems to think that certain students are Apsyn infiltrators." Felyx flipped the page and then set the folder down on the table between them and fanned out the next several pages, which were information on a handful of students.

One of those students Ax recognized, and his heart lurched. "There's got to be some mistake." He pointed at Luci's picture and then looked over at Felyx. "There's no way that the Apsyns would use a human."

And certainly not Luci. She would die before becoming an Apsyn spy. But he held that back for the moment. He didn't know what Felyx knew about her, and he didn't want to reveal all of her secrets without her permission.

Though the information about what had been done to her was known by the Synnr military. There was no way to avoid that. He didn't know how much of her file Felyx had read, but anyone with sense would recognize that Luci was innocent.

"It'd be kind of genius if they did use her or one

of the other humans." Felyx nodded to another picture of a human. The rest of the pictures were Zulir, though Ax didn't really recognize any of them.

"Genius? They don't think humans are capable. They would never use one like this." It wasn't just about Luci's past. Ax had seen the disdain Apsyns had for humans firsthand. To them, humans were beasts incapable of higher thought.

"I'm sure they think animals can be trained. And Apsyns know we would never think they would hire human. Or brainwash one. This girl spent some time on Kilrym. Plenty of time for them to get inside her head and mess with it." Felyx said it with the dispassion of someone who barely thought about humans at all.

It made Ax's blood boil. "Humans aren't animals."

"I know that." Felyx did not sound pleased and he gave Ax a sharp look. "I'm saying that the Apsyns think of them as animals. Follow along."

Ax was following along just fine. And if he followed along any closer he might punch his partner. "The Apsyns treated Luci terribly. All of the humans that were recovered from that mission were treated terribly. None of them have kind thoughts for the Apsyns. She needs to be taken off the list. She's not an Apsyn infiltrator."

"They had her for months," Felyx countered. "They could have gotten inside her brain and on whatever they wanted. I'm not saying that she's guilty. I'm saying that she might not know what she's doing."

"That's thinking pretty far ahead, even for the Apsyns. It's been six months since she came here. And she wasn't even in the Red Building two days ago." What would make Felyx understand? Why wasn't this obvious?

"The Apsyns are capable of thinking ahead."

"Not this far. She's not the infiltrator." Ax would bet his life on it.

"Are you thinking with your head or with your cock?" Felyx accused, eyes narrowed and arms crossed.

"Excuse me?" This had nothing to do with his relationship with Luci. And Ax wanted to slug Felyx for even suggesting it.

"This is war. We need to be thinking clearly."

"And assuming a traumatized woman would betray her people and her home is not thinking clearly." Why did Felyx not understand that? Maybe it was because Ax knew the humans better than Felyx. As far as he knew, Felyx had never met them. But Ax was certain. None of them would turn on the Synnrs.

But Felyx refused to take him at his word. "If you say she's not the infiltrator, find a way to prove it.

There are a dozen suspects. At least one of them is working for the Apsyns."

Ax seethed as they went through the rest of the information. How was he supposed to prove that someone *wasn't* working for the Apsyns? He could not prove a negative.

Especially when it was so ridiculous to even think it.

He would simply have to find the Apsyn infiltrator himself.

He memorized the faces of every suspect, even the other human, though he doubted the Apsyns would actually use a human. He was going to figure out who it was and clear Luci's name.

She was his to protect.

8

Ax: It's completely safe to go back to school. I scared the Apsyns away.

Luci: LOL

Ax: What does that mean?

Luci: Never mind. I'm sure your big, scary muscles did the trick. But maybe I should take another look at them just to be sure.

Ax: (attached, a picture of his big, scary muscles)

BY THE END of math class, Luci had herself all tied in knots, half convinced that Hanna was a secret Apsyn spy who had come to campus to sabotage everything.

It couldn't be true. It couldn't.

Right?

Luci didn't pay attention to the lesson, and she knew she would regret that later. Thankfully the professor hadn't done anything too complex. He seemed to be very aware that his students were still mentally recovering from the events on campus two days before and had used most of the class as a review session.

Still, Luci didn't know if she was going to remember a single thing. Not when she was so busy thinking about Hanna.

Why would she be an Apsyn spy? That was the question that Luci kept coming back to. An Apsyn spy would not befriend a human.

Or maybe they would just to throw off the scent.

Luci screamed internally at her circular logic. But she couldn't rule out the fact that she was suspecting Hanna of something.

At the very least, she was acting suspicious.

Was she? A voice in the back of Luci's head asked. Or was Hanna just as messed up as Luci was since they had both been on campus during the attack.

Luci wanted the logical voice in the back of her head to come up with an explanation or shut the fuck up. She didn't like feeling all at loose ends.

She considered sending Ax a message about Hanna, but stopped herself. She didn't want to be a snitch.

Though was it snitching when you were talking

about possible espionage?

Espionage?

That was a bit far. She just thought Hanna was suspicious, she couldn't be a real spy. This wasn't a James Bond movie, and even with war brewing all around them, Luci couldn't believe that Hanna had anything to do with it.

Hanna was sneaking out of the classroom.

Okay, she wasn't sneaking, but she was leaving furtively along with all the other students. Luci's imagination was running wild, and she needed to get a hold of herself.

Luci followed her. She didn't do it on purpose at first. There were half a dozen paths Luci could take that branched off, and she and Hanna just happened to be going in the same direction.

But then Hanna took a detour towards the Red Building, and Luci's suspicions were pinged even further. That place was off-limits while campus security and the Synnr soldiers were doing an investigation. Why would Hanna want to go in there?

It could have been curiosity. She was a person the same as Luci, and people were curious. But that didn't give her the right to sneak into a secured area.

Luci knew that this was definitely the point to call Ax and tell him what was going on.

But she didn't do that. If Hanna wasn't a spy,

she'd get in trouble for venturing into this building, and Luci didn't want to be the cause of that, not if she could help it. She needed a better idea of what Hanna was really thinking.

She followed Hanna into the building to see what she was doing. Maybe she just had to get something from one of the rooms. There were storage lockers that the students could use in the Red Building, and it was perfectly reasonable for Hanna to want to sneak inside and get something that belonged to her.

But Hanna walked right past the lockers and headed up the stairs.

Now was the time for Luci to turn back. She'd conjured a good reason for Hanna to be in the building and it had just gone up in smoke. She didn't have to turn Hanna in, but she shouldn't go any further. Luci knew that, but she couldn't force herself to turn around. She was in too deep to go back.

Her blood fizzed with excitement, and she could feel her hands tremble with the knowledge that she was in a forbidden area and that she would get in a lot of trouble if she was caught.

They might even think that she had something to do with the Apsyn incursion.

And *that* would be ridiculous. Clearly Luci was not an Apsyn spy.

With that reassurance in mind, she continued following Hanna. Someone would understand that

Luci would never be a spy. Ax would believe her. He was her—well, she wasn't going to think about that at the moment.

She wasn't sure if even she believed that excuse, but she really wanted to keep going.

It was eerily silent in the building, and Luci had to hang back pretty far to keep from being spotted. She wondered why there wasn't any security inside the building, but was thankful that it meant that she wasn't at even greater risk of being caught.

And then Hanna ducked into a room that looked like it had been ransacked.

Was this where Ax had fought off the Apsyns? She remembered the way his skin had been so disgustingly singed with an Apsyn's spark, and she wished she had powers of her own just so she could hunt that Apsyn down and hurt them the way they had hurt her boy—her *friend*.

But she wasn't thinking about Ax right now. She was focusing on Hanna and whatever suspicious stuff Hanna was doing.

Hanna gave the area where the fight had taken place a wide berth and headed straight for a small locker right next to the teacher's desk.

If Hanna turned around, she would see Luci. Luci realized that about two seconds before Hanna paused where she stood and listened for something, as if she could sense that Luci was right there.

Luci froze. She feared if she moved the tiniest bit that Hanna would see her. Then Hanna started moving again and Luci ducked behind the door to give herself a bit of cover.

She could still see what was going on, but hopefully Hanna wouldn't notice her.

Hanna opened the locker—or was it a safe—pretty easily and read through a short stack of papers. Then she almost surprised a gasp out of Luci by the unleashing her spark and burning the papers to cinders.

What the hell was she doing? That was majorly suspicious.

And Hanna was heading for the door. Luci backed up and looked around for an avenue of escape. But they were several feet from the stairwell and Hanna was sure to spot her.

Luci dove into a darkened classroom and ducked behind a table, hoping that Hanna did not investigate.

She didn't.

Luci stayed in the classroom for several minutes, her heart pounding wildly as she tried to make sense of what she had just seen.

What was on those papers? What was Hanna doing?

Did she need to tell Ax about this?

It was super suspicious. And Luci didn't know if

there were spies on campus, but she had read enough books and seen enough TV shows to know that spies were everywhere. At least back on Earth that seemed true in fiction, but never in real life.

Once she had managed to calm her racing heart and had listened for several moments to make sure that Hanna wasn't right outside, Luci carefully got to her feet and crept out of the classroom.

She walked cautiously through the building and retraced her steps down the staircase and out the little door that Hanna had used as an entrance. Luckily, Hanna wasn't anywhere to be seen. But the same could not be said for Ax. He caught her as she closed the door quietly behind her, his face a mask of betrayed fury.

"What in Braznon's bowels are you doing here?"

***

LUCI'S CHEEKS BLUSHED CRIMSON, and at any other moment Ax might have thought it was cute. But he wanted to unleash his spark and send off a blast somewhere as a way to funnel his fury at what he was seeing.

What was she doing in the Red Building? It was off-limits. He had just spent the last hour trying to convince Felyx that Luci wasn't suspicious, and here she was being suspicious.

"Well?" he demanded again. "What are you doing here?" He looked around and noticed that they were in a pretty open area. It was pure luck that Luci hadn't yet been seen coming out of the building. And pure luck that he was the one who'd caught her.

He grabbed her by the arm and tugged her around the corner, where they were obscured by the shadows cast by the Red Building. They were off the main walking path and *slightly* less likely to be noticed.

He hoped. He could imagine the look on Felyx's face if he heard that Luci had been snooping, and he didn't know how he would defend her again.

"Why were you in there?" he asked again. Luci hadn't said anything, and the longer she went in silence, the more concerned he grew.

She couldn't actually be a spy, could she? No. Absolutely not. Even if he'd seen her talking to the person in charge of the Apsyn espionage division and being handed direct orders, Ax wouldn't believe it. He knew Luci, and he knew what line she wouldn't cross.

"Why do you care?" Luci asked with surprising vehemence. She looked over his shoulder as if she was looking for someone, but he wasn't about to let her escape until he understood what she was doing and why.

What kind of game was she playing? "This area is

forbidden." Everyone knew that. There was a large sign on the door that said it. And there should have been a security alert any time someone went in the building. Ax would need to investigate whether the alarm had actually sounded or if something had malfunctioned with the system.

"So?" Luci really wasn't helping to exonerate herself of any suspicion.

Ax felt like he was going crazy. He wanted to help; he wanted to do what it took to keep Luci free of suspicion. But to do that, he needed the facts. "It's my job to keep this place safe." He didn't want to accuse her of anything. Was she really going to make him? He was still angry, but it was all a mishmash of seeing Luci where she wasn't supposed to be and remembering the horrible words that Felyx had said.

Luci scoffed. "From me? Come on." She rolled her eyes at him as if it was the most ludicrous suggestion he could make.

And Ax didn't know what made him say it, but he did, even knowing it would hurt her. Maybe it was the shock she needed to get her act together. "Apparently you've been acting suspicious."

"What's that supposed to mean?" Luci crossed her arms and jutted her chin out in challenge.

It was a complete breach of protocol to tell her what he'd learned in the briefing. But he was absolutely certain she wasn't the spy. And it wasn't like he was going to tell her the other people that had come up in Felyx's investigation.

Just her.

Just so she knew.

Felyx would say he wasn't using his brain, but Ax knew he was right. And this wasn't him thinking with his cock. If he didn't want security forces looking more closely at Luci, then she needed to know that they were looking at her in the first place so that she stopped acting weird.

It all made sense in his head. He just hoped he wouldn't need to explain himself to a supervisor. "Some people think the Apsyns are using you to infiltrate campus." He didn't want to go so far as to accuse her of being a spy. That would cross the line.

"What?" Luci threw her hands up, and for a second Ax wondered if she was going to hit him, but she just waved them around for a second before crossing them and glaring at him.

"I didn't say I believed them." He wanted that to be very clear. He was on Luci's side. She was his… friend. And he knew exactly what the Apsyns had done to her. He would never in a million years consider that she would betray the Synnrs.

"That's crazy," she said, arms crossed even tighter, as if she was shrinking into herself.

"I know that," he wanted to reassure her, but she was

still coming out of a forbidden area and she wouldn't tell him why. "So why are you coming out of there?" He nodded towards the Red Building. "It's suspicious."

She groaned and protested. "No, it's not. I'm not a spy. You know that."

"Do I?" The words slipped out, and Ax regretted saying them the moment they hit the air.

"You should." She winced, and her eyes watered in anger. She was hurt.

And something possessed Ax to dig himself even deeper into this hole. Luci wasn't reacting like he expected, and it was throwing him off. She was purposefully keeping him at arm's length and ignoring the rules while he was doing everything it took to keep her safe. "Why should I? It's not like I really know that much about you."

Luci's eyes widened. "Excuse me?" Her hands uncrossed and landed on her hips.

He shouldn't have said that. He should have stopped talking a long time ago and should have just gotten Luci's reason for being in the Red Building. But Luci was angry, and so was he. And he was starting to realize that he wasn't asking her about being a spy. That wasn't what he wanted to know about her. That wasn't his issue.

And maybe Felyx had been right about him thinking too much with his cock.

Ax couldn't stop himself from adding, "You don't want anyone to know you. To get close."

She was shaking her head as he spoke. "That's not true."

"So it's just me?" Clearly some outside force had taken hold of his mouth, because Ax could not believe the things he was saying.

"What?" He was lucky she didn't have a spark, because she would have definitely lashed out by this point and singed him to the core.

"Never mind." He was so far out of bounds that he was lucky she hadn't hit him.

It was everything coming to a head. His meeting with Felyx. The attack on the University. The fact that Luci wanted to keep space between them. Space that she had every right to keep between them.

Space that he wished didn't exist.

"Maybe you don't deserve to know me," Luci said. And then she stormed off, not bothering to even say goodbye.

Ax deserved it. But as she left, he realized that she hadn't told him why she'd gone in the building. Was something up with her? He would need to check the security feed to see what was going on.

No matter what, he did not believe that Luci was a spy. But something was going on, and he had to figure out what.

9

Luci: I just realized I'm never going to see the Grand Canyon. It's stupid to be sad about that.

Ax: It's not stupid.

Luci: I should stop pretending that I'll ever get my old life back. Maybe it's time to do something about it.

Ax: Like what?

Ax had some freaking nerve. Luci wanted to scream in frustration, but she held it inside. Was that the healthiest response? Probably not. But she didn't really give two shits about being healthy at the moment.

Where did Ax get off on saying that? She wasn't his girlfriend. And she wasn't a spy.

How dare he.

How freaking dare he.

Though maybe she should have told him why she was in the building. She screwed her face up at the thought. He did have a job to do. And the Red Building was off-limits.

God dammit. She couldn't even hold onto her anger for more than thirty seconds. This was bullshit.

But she wasn't about to turn around and go apologize to him or explain herself. Not after what he'd said.

He didn't own her. He had no rights to her. She hadn't given him any.

And it didn't matter if her stupid emotions got a little bit confused sometimes when it came to him. She was an adult, and she was living her life and figuring things out on her own.

The confrontation almost scrubbed the question of what Hanna was doing out of Luci's mind. *That* was definitely something she needed to tell Ax, even if she was mad at him.

But she could do that later. She didn't really think that Hanna was a spy or anything like that, but she had been acting suspicious. Maybe Ax would know why.

Or maybe she was about to snitch on a friend as a peace offering to a friend with benefits.

Luci groaned. Why was adulthood so hard?

She caught sight of Hanna and almost called out

to say hi. Maybe Hanna could explain why she had been in the Red Building.

But something stopped Luci from saying anything. She was supposed to be heading towards the bus stop to catch a ride home. That was the main reason students took this path. But Hanna didn't look like she was heading toward a vehicle or any other transportation option.

She took a turn and headed deeper into campus.

She was a student. That was probably fine. But she had been acting suspicious in the Red Building. And it wouldn't hurt to just have an idea of what she was doing.

Luci wasn't sure what possessed her to follow Hanna, but she did it anyway.

Hanna headed to the edge of campus where the aerospace building and vehicles were located.

Not necessarily strange, but Luci didn't know if Hanna was taking any aerospace engineering courses or anything that would give her a reason to be in this area. If she was in some sort of aerospace program, why would she be taking an entry level math class?

But unlike the Red Building, it wasn't completely off-limits.

Still, Luci hung back far enough so Hanna couldn't see her. She was acting suspicious, and Luci didn't want to give away her position. Either Hanna would be mad at her for following her... stalking her… Or she might have a different reaction if she actually was a spy.

Which was still ridiculous.

But nothing she was doing seemed completely innocent.

Of course, after Luci's conversation with Ax, everything seemed suspicious.

Conversation? Okay, it was an argument, one Luci had run away from rather than see through to the end.

Hanna stopped near a small building that looked like a storage shed. Luci didn't know what it was for, but it didn't look like something that students would be using.

Hanna looked left and right. Luci had to duck out of sight for a minute to avoid being seen. But then Hanna summoned her spark and shot it directly at the door to that small outbuilding.

Definitely shady. There was no good reason to be blasting locks off doors. That was *not* a legitimate activity.

What was Hanna doing? Why was she breaking in?

Luci couldn't get any closer if she wanted to keep from being seen. She wished she had binoculars or some kind of enhanced vision. All she had was her communicator.

But it did have a camera with zoom feature.

Luckily, the communicators on Aorsa were really similar to smart phones back on Earth. They had more features and the holograms were cool, but they were basically operated in the same fashion.

She pulled out her communicator and held it up in front of her, zooming in as best she could. She could make out shadows in the doorway of the building that Hanna had snuck into, but other than that she couldn't see much.

About a minute later, Hanna came out of that building holding a heavy duffel bag with some wires sticking out of the top.

Hanna must have noticed them too, since she took a moment to shove them in the bag before fastening it shut.

Okay, that was not good. That could *not* be good.

Was she stealing technology?

Was this spy stuff?

Was she a thief from a rival school?

There were a lot of possibilities, but Luci didn't think any of them reflected well on Hanna.

This would be the time to call Ax, or if she was still super mad at him any of the other security guards roaming the campus.

But she still felt like Hanna was her friend and she didn't want to rat her out.

She knew she was gonna regret that. She had a vague memory of watching older kids steal candy from the local gas station when she was little. She hadn't wanted to tell on them either, and she had ended up grounded for a week when someone noticed a bunch of candy wrappers in the garbage.

But she wasn't a little kid anymore, and this was a big deal. If Hanna wasn't a spy or a criminal, she could end up in big trouble over a misunderstanding. Luci didn't want that to happen.

Hanna kept moving toward the aerospace area, but she didn't go into the building.

There were several spaceships of varying sizes behind the building. The casual way Synnrs approached space travel was still shocking to Luci, even after months. Just about anyone could be licensed to pilot a spacefaring vehicle. It was no more shocking than a human back on Earth having a driver's license.

That took some getting used to. Luci remembered seeing spaceships on TV when she was a little girl. She had seen videos of the moon landing and things like that. The idea that spaceships could just be parked in a parking lot and launched into orbit with the press of a few buttons still boggled her mind.

But she figured she'd get used to it. Eventually.

Most of the ships that the school owned had identification numbers painted in broad strokes on their sides. But one of them didn't have numbers.

Luci didn't know if it wasn't oversight or if that ship didn't belong to the school.

And that was the one Hanna went to.

Suspicious, suspicious, suspicious.

Luci really should call in some backup. She knew that. And she was cursing herself, but it was like something else inside of her head took over and she had to see this through by herself.

She could regret it later. If she lived long enough for that to happen.

Hanna opened the side hatch to the ship and placed the large duffel bag inside.

Luci stepped forward to get a better look, her communicator still in front of her, the zoom fully engaged.

She was so busy looking at the screen that she didn't pay attention to the ground in front of her, and she stumbled over a large rock in her path.

"Ouch!"

She didn't mean to say it. It was definitely an accident. But it was enough to gain Hanna's attention.

The woman spun around, her wings flaring wide as she saw Luci.

And for the first time, Luci was really afraid. Maybe this was the moment to yell and scream for help. But they were in a far off edge of campus. No one would hear her.

"What are you doing here?" Hanna demanded as she stalked closer. Her spread wings made her look like some sort of avenging angel intent on striking down her foe.

"I—um... I—" Luci couldn't figure out what to say. There was no explanation that would get her out of the situation.

"You shouldn't have followed me," said Hanna. And she sounded regretful.

Luci didn't like her tone. Why did Hanna need to be regretful? "I wasn't following you," Luci lied. Poorly. Why had she never learned to fib?

Hanna's wings flared. "Don't lie to me, girl."

Girl. Why did everybody come back to the age thing. Luci had been through more in her 19 years than most people in their whole lives.

Hanna's wings brightened, and Luci realized she was about to be struck by her spark. She didn't want that. And before Hanna could strike out, Luci dropped to the ground and rolled forward, dropping her communicator in the process.

Hanna didn't expect it. And she certainly wasn't ready when Luci came up and slugged her across the face.

Ow. That really hurt. Who would have known that faces were so bony.

Luci wasn't going to mess with punches anymore.

Those really hurt. So she kicked out and managed to land a blow against Hanna's knee.

But the surprise wore off quickly. Hanna punched her back, and Luci actually felt her lip split open.

She stumbled to the ground as the taste of copper bloomed in her mouth.

"You should have never gotten involved, human. I am sorry about this."

The last thing Luci saw was a bright flash of white.

AX WAS ROOTED in place for about a minute trying to think of the proper response to everything Luci had said. And everything he'd said to her.

He needed to apologize. He was out of line. And yes, he needed answers about why she was in the Red Building, but he also needed to make sure that things were okay between them. He knew that she wasn't the spy. Nothing could make her spy for the Apsyns.

And it was also abundantly obvious that they hadn't been talking about spying.

They were talking about the relationship.

And that was something they really did need to talk about.

Ax wasn't sure that he could keep up the charade that he didn't feel anything but lust for her. He wanted a real relationship, one where she came to him with her problems and they solved them together. But if Luci didn't want that, he would have to live with it.

He needed to talk to her first. They needed to have that conversation.

He finally took off, heading in the same direction she went. He figured she was going to catch a bus to get back to her place, and he wanted to catch her before she left campus. The longer they waited to talk, the worse things would be.

But she wasn't at the bus depot. That was kind of strange.

He checked the schedule posted by the bench where commuters could wait for the bus and saw that there were still several minutes until the next bus would come. She hadn't had a chance to get on one already.

Had she found another ride home?

That was possible. She could have called a taxi.

He pulled out his communicator with the thought that he could send her a message, just to make sure she was okay.

And at first he was confused at what he was seeing. It was a video message. A Zulir student was apparently breaking into a small outbuilding and taking a large bag from it. Then she continued on toward the aerospace area.

The message came from Luci's communicator.

Was she intentionally sending him a message? Or had she accidentally engaged the video call?

He didn't know. But at least now he had an idea of where Luci was.

Who was the student? And what was she doing?

Ax's stomach churned at what he was seeing on the video. He didn't like the idea of Luci following someone when he knew there were Apsyn infiltrators on the campus.

He especially didn't like it when the woman with the bag turned around and flared her wings.

There was a scuffle and the communicator fell to the ground. Ax had seen enough. He took off running. Luci was in danger and the other woman was up to no good.

Ax sprinted toward the aerospace area. Luci needed help. The thought echoed through his mind with every step. He wasn't moving fast enough; light speed wouldn't be fast enough. But he had to keep moving.

He made it past the outbuilding with the broken door and toward the area where all of the campus space vehicles were parked.

There was no sign of Luci or the other woman. Not at first.

But a glint of something reflective caught his eye, and he saw that it was Luci's communicator laying on the ground. He picked it up and shoved it in his pocket.

Luci had been here. And if she didn't have her communicator with her, it meant that nothing good was going on.

Was the other woman gone? Had she done something to Luci?

He spotted a vehicle that was out of place. All of the school vehicles had identification numbers written on their sides. But one of the vehicles in the parking area was not marked.

That vehicle did not belong to the University of Aorsa.

So what was it doing here?

And why was it starting up?

It took several minutes to ready a vehicle for space flight, and it was strange to think that a vehicle would be launching without anyone from the campus around to observe it.

Ax would bet all that he was worth that the woman who had hurt Luci was on that vehicle.

Was Luci on that vehicle too? He didn't know why someone would want to abduct a student in the middle of carrying out a theft, but since he didn't see Luci anywhere else, he had to check there first.

The rear hatch of the vehicle was still open, and

he dashed across the lot as fast as he could and scampered on.

With the sound of the engines engaging and all of the other industrial equipment going, he doubted that the pilot of the vehicle could hear him.

The vehicle was small as spacefaring vessels went, but all spacefaring vessels were larger than land bound vehicles. He couldn't immediately see if Luci was stuck somewhere in the cargo bay. There were lots of crates and storage nooks to search.

Ax knew he didn't have much time, but he was going to take every second that he could.

And he finally found her stashed away in a corner, hidden in a box with a faulty latch.

Ax had to use his spark to pop it open all the way, and when he saw Luci's face, he wanted to roar in fury.

She had been beaten. There was a nasty bruise forming on her cheek and blood trailed from her lip. He saw that her knuckles were also a mess, bruised and bloodied.

She had fought back.

It made him proud to think it, but he still wanted to murder anyone who had dared to lay hands on her.

He didn't see any sign of the large bag that he had witnessed the woman steal from Luci's video.

Then again, he hadn't really been looking for it,

too preoccupied with finding Luci.

Luci was pretty out of it, but he managed to get her out of the crate. She wasn't completely unconscious, but she wasn't coherent. He doubted she would cling to him as tightly if she could think about what she was doing. Still, Ax held on. Feeling her in his arms was no reassurance that everything would work out, but it was physical proof that she was alive.

As long as she was alive, they could figure things out. As long as she was alive, he could apologize for how he'd screwed up. But that wasn't the priority at the moment. Right now he had to get Luci moving and to somewhere safe.

He managed to get her on her feet and they stumbled towards the cargo bay doors.

But before they could cross the full length of the cargo bay, the doors began to close.

Ax tried to pick up the pace, but Luci stumbled, her feet dragging along the floor. And by the time they had righted themselves, the doors had closed with a clang.

Beside him Luci shuddered and started talking, her words a bit slurred. "What's going on? Where are we?"

Ax could answer that question.

But the more important one was where were they going?

Ax: I'll take you on a new adventure.

LUCI'S HEAD ached and she tried to roll to her side, as if that would do something to stop the pain. Instead it intensified, throbbing and spreading throughout her skull. She groaned and felt something soft and yet firm right by her head.

"You're okay. You're okay." She knew that voice. She really liked that voice.

That voice shouldn't be here right now.

She cracked her eyes open, and the first thing she saw was industrial metal and then the sleeve of Ax's uniform.

Was she in prison? Was he holding her hostage?

Her mind was kind of fuzzy. She couldn't remember what just happened or why she'd been asleep. She blinked a few times, as if that would clear the cobwebs from her head. Asleep or unconscious?

She didn't know.

But Ax wasn't holding her hostage. That was crazy. She managed to sit up and her head spun a little. Though the pain in her head was her primary concern, she was starting to feel all the other little aches and annoyances throughout the rest of her body.

She was hurt. Big time hurt. She tasted copper on her lip and teased the cut that ran along part of her mouth. She winced as she did it. That didn't feel good. For some reason, she couldn't stop herself though. It was like it was grounding her in the moment.

There was a rumbling sound all around them, and Luci couldn't tell what it was. Where *were* they? How had she gotten here? At first the memories refused to come, but she wasn't going to give up. It came back in flashes. The fight with Ax. Following Hanna. The duffel bag. The spaceship.

They were on the spaceship.

Luci jerked up and tried to move, but Ax held her in place. That made her head throb even more, but her panic made her neurons go crazy, and the pain was the last thing she was worried about.

"Don't move too fast. Just breathe." He spoke calmly and his hands were warm. At any other time

Luci would have loved it, but not now. She wanted out.

"What's going on? Where are we going? We need to get out of here." Her mind flashed back to being held by the Apsyns. She didn't remember being abducted from Earth or the long space journey after that. She had been put into cryosleep for most of it. She wouldn't have survived the long trek otherwise. But it might have been something like this.

Luci tried to breathe, but her breath came too fast, and her heartbeat was so rapid that she worried it would explode.

That was crazy talk. That wasn't going to happen. Ax was right there with her. They could get out of this thing.

She took a moment to get her bearings. The engines of the ship were going, but she couldn't feel the vehicle moving at all. She hoped that meant that they hadn't yet taken off. If they were still on the ground, they could get off of the ship.

They appeared to be in a cargo bay of some kind. The doors were closed, but doors were meant to be opened. They could do that.

"How long have I been out?" She didn't know if it mattered in the grand scheme of things, but it felt important right now. It felt like something she could have control over.

"I don't think you've been out for very long. We

were… It's only been about fifteen minutes, maybe half an hour since we last spoke." He said it carefully, like he didn't want her to remember what they had last spoken about.

But Luci remembered the fight. And rather than feel angry about it, she was glad to know that Ax had come right after her. She didn't know if he wanted to apologize or if there was something else, but he hadn't let her flounder.

"Let's get out of here and I can thank you for saving me once we're back at your place." She tried to inject a bit of humor and a bit of sexiness into the offer.

But Ax's face was grim. "Don't—let's just try to get out of here."

What did he mean by that? Did he not want her anymore? Now was *not* the time to have that argument. Or discussion. If he didn't want anything going on between them, it wouldn't really be an argument.

She finally got to her feet alongside Ax and they both made their way towards the cargo bay door. The most obvious thing to try was to press the button to open the door, but that did nothing.

"They lock in preparation for takeoff," said Ax as he pressed the button again with more vigor, as if that would change the situation. His face had gone hard and Luci saw the soldier in him come out.

"Okay, then we'll have to try something else then," Luci said. She pressed against the door as hard as she could. She wasn't surprised when it did nothing. She threw herself at it and her shoulder protested the abuse.

Her shoulder would learn to deal with it. If they didn't get off this ship, they were in deep trouble. Luci didn't want to think about where they might be going or what could happen to them. She just had to stay focused on the moment.

She found a fairly large piece of metal and picked it up to try and use it to pry the door open. When she gripped the metal tight, the cuts on her knuckles from her fight with Hanna burst open and fresh blood started to pool. Luci ignored it. She never considered herself the kind of person who could easily ignore pain, but in this situation she had no other choice.

The metal wedged in between the two bay doors, but it didn't do anything to get them open. They didn't budge an inch.

"Is there some sort of emergency override?" That seemed like the kind of safety feature that there should be. Like an emergency brake on a car.

"I don't know," Ax responded with a grunt as he searched around on his half of the cargo bay for something that might work. "It would probably be hidden behind a hatch of some kind if it's there," he said. "Wouldn't hurt to look."

She didn't know if he was just humoring her, and at the moment she didn't care. She needed to do *something*. Luci stared at the portion of wall closest to the door and ran her hands over it, looking for a secret hatch that would have an emergency kill switch.

There was nothing.

She cursed.

They were going to die. There was no other way around it. Whether it happened in space or on Kilrym or because Hanna caught them, they were entering into the last minutes of their lives.

This wasn't how Luci wanted to die. She was just starting her life over again.

No. She couldn't give up hope yet. The ship wasn't even off the ground. They just had to look harder. She redoubled her efforts, pressing harder against the metal panels of the cargo bay hull and looking for anything that might save them.

Ax wasn't looking for a switch. He had unleashed his wings and was hurling his spark at the door. Apparently the ship was designed to absorb the electricity that came from Zulir wings, since it seemed to have no effect on the ship.

God damnit.

Ax gave a yell of fury and threw himself at the

door, going so far as to punch it, as if that would do anything. Then he pulled his hand back with a yelp and Luci could see the blood starting to pool.

She rushed away from where she was and looked for something that would clean the wound. It looked kind of nasty.

She grabbed his hand with her own, and her own bloody knuckles brushed against the cut.

Luci froze in place as their wounds touched, and then her vision went white.

A MATCH.

Luci was his Match.

The awareness ripped through Ax and rewrote his knowledge of himself. Luci wasn't just some woman he was attracted to. She wasn't just a human that he had helped to rescue when she needed it.

She was his destiny.

It felt like they were frozen together for an eternity, but he came back to himself with a jerky breath. The ship was still starting up, and they were still stuck in the cargo bay looking for a way out. Nothing about their situation had changed.

But everything was different. He hadn't expected it to happen like this. He hadn't expected it at all, but there was no time to dwell. Not while their lives were in danger.

Luci's eyes had gone wide, and she stared at him in wonder.

"What..." She didn't even finish the question.

"Later." It hurt Ax to even suggest it, but they didn't have time to deal with the ramifications of being a Matched pair. It didn't change anything. They weren't bonded. Luci still didn't want him that way. And even if they did seal the bond between them, it didn't mean that anything romantic had to happen. Plenty of bonded pairs were not romantically involved.

But really, he shouldn't be thinking of romance at all at the moment. They were stuck in a spaceship in the cargo bay and possibly headed toward space at any moment. He hadn't said anything yet, but there was no guarantee that the cargo bay would have sufficient life support for both of them. If they launched, they might run out of oxygen very quickly.

"Are we..." Luci didn't finish the question.

"We're going to get out of here," Ax said. That was all he could focus on at the moment.

But no matter what each of them did, they couldn't get the doors to budge. The button didn't work. There was no emergency kill switch. It was just the two of them stuck in the cargo bay with no way out.

"Do cargo bays get life support?" Luci asked as another engine fired, a sure sign that takeoff would be coming at any moment. Of course she would ask. She was smart enough to figure it out on her own.

"I don't know." He wasn't going to lie to her.

"Will it hurt to…" She couldn't finish the question, and she swiped at an eye quickly, wiping away a tear before she could begin to cry in earnest.

But he was pretty sure he knew what she was going to ask. Would it hurt to die that way? Ax didn't know for sure. But he didn't want her even more afraid. "It wouldn't hurt," he said. He'd much rather die in battle than in a metal coffin, but at least he'd have Luci beside him. It wasn't a consolation. He would sacrifice his life without a thought if it meant getting her off this ship.

She didn't look like she believed him. He didn't believe himself.

There was a hatch to the main part of the ship, but it would lead right to where Hanna was piloting. This wasn't the kind of ship with crew quarters or a ton of hidden areas that they could sneak into. It was meant for short hauls between Aorsa and Kilrym. There was no place to hide. But they could try the door.

"Can we use your communicator to call for help?" Maybe someone wouldn't get there in time, but they'd at least know that she and Ax had been taken.

Ax looked at his communicator and his face fell. "Something is interfering with the signal. And once we're off Aorsa, it won't work. This type of communicator doesn't work between Aorsa and Kilrym." He nodded towards the front of the ship. "We can let her know we're here," Ax offered. If Hanna was an Apsyn spy, then it would blow any chance the Synnrs had of finding her. And of finding out what she was planning to do. But they might survive.

Luci seemed to consider it for a moment, and then she shook her head from side to side in the way that the humans did. "No. You said there might be a spy. Hanna is acting weird. She stole something. She's on a spaceship. If she's heading to Kilrym to give the Apsyns something, then we need to see if we can stop her or at least figure out what she's doing."

Pride warred with concern at Luci's bravery. "That's not your job. Not your responsibility. I can't ask you to put yourself in danger like that." He wanted her safe on Aorsa. He wanted her far away from any possible danger ever.

But Luci gave him a small smile and hugged him close. "You're not the one putting me in danger. You came to rescue me." She kissed his cheek. "We're not going to die. There's going to be life support and we'll figure out what we're going to do when we get there. Wherever there is."

With this kind of ship, the only *there* possible was Kilrym or a space station.

Another engine engaged. "We don't have much time. We need to secure ourselves as best as we can."

There were two seats in the cargo bay which Ax took as a good sign that the cargo bay was at least capable of sustaining life support. He and Luci strapped themselves in and they clasped hands, holding on tightly as they considered what was about to happen.

And a moment later the ship took off, carrying them to an unknown destination and to their possible death.

---

*Luci: **When** I can't sleep, I pretend that someone's holding me tight.*

*Ax: **Does** it help?*

*Luci: **Sometimes.** When it's…*

Ax: ?

Luci: (no response)

LUCI'S HEAD rang with the prospect that Ax was her mate. **Match.** Whatever. She wasn't exactly clear on what the difference between a mate and a Match was, and it seemed to only matter to the Synnrs. Was this why she couldn't get him out of her head? Was this why she didn't want to?

It was better to think about that than the possibility that they were about to die as soon as the ship rocketed into space. Ax gripped her hand tight enough to hurt, but she didn't tell him to stop. He was the only connection she had to reality, and she was going to cling to him as long as he would let her.

It got louder and louder, and then with a rumble and shake, the ship took off. Luci held her breath as if that would make some kind of a difference. She didn't know if she was doing it on purpose or not, but after a moment she forced herself to let it out.

And then she took in another breath and another.

Her ears popped, but she kept breathing, and the longer the ship flew the more certain she was that the life support had engaged.

They were alive. They had survived this one little hurdle. There was still the question of where they were going and what would be meeting them when they got there, but they would have to deal with that then.

And maybe at some point in the future, Luci would have to really question what it meant to be Ax's Match.

Was she happy about it? Upset? Indifferent?

No, not indifferent. She couldn't quite grasp what the emotion was churning around in her stomach, but it definitely wasn't indifference.

"I was in the Red Building because I followed Hanna there," she said. It was a little belated, but if they were going to survive whatever was about to be thrown at them, Ax needed the full story.

He didn't let go of her hand, and she gripped him so tight that she wasn't letting it go without a fight. "I figured that out," he replied. "Is that why you sent me the video?"

"What video?" She hadn't sent him a video. Well not recently, and not a video that they were supposed to talk about when they weren't alone in a bedroom somewhere.

"The video of Hanna breaking into that storage facility and hurting you." There was an emphasis on what Hanna had done to her that Luci was afraid to decipher.

Of course Ax wouldn't want to see her hurt. He was a good man. But there was more to it than that.

Luci hadn't sent him anything on purpose, but apparently she'd hit a wrong button or two and that had sent him running her way. She was happy for the error. "Do you think she's working with the Apsyns?" Luci hated to think it, but she had been thinking it ever since Hanna stole the duffel bag, beat her up, and threw her on the ship.

"I think that's a possibility. What do you know about her?" Ax asked. He let go of her hand for a moment, and Luci felt the loss. Ax unbuckled himself and grabbed the med kit off the wall, opening it up and then kneeling before her and applying healing cream to her wounds as she spoke. She could feel it working, the little aches and pains she was trying to ignore melting away under the onslaught of his touch.

A moment later, he was back in his seat and holding her hand as if nothing had happened.

Luci racked her brain, thinking through the few conversations that she had had with Hanna. "I… We have math class together. We talked about the assignments and joked about them. And… She is… I don't know anything about her." Why had Luci considered Hanna a friend? Was she so desperate for any sort of connection that she was willing to cling to one of the few people who was open and nice to her?

And what did that say about Ax?

Nope. Not going there.

"You don't know anything?"

"You don't have to say it like that." Luci wasn't a spy hunter. Of course she didn't have in-depth information about her fellow students.

"I'm not saying it like anything."

"Then you should listen to your tone."

Ax smiled as she glared at him, and while at some point that might have made her angry, this time it made her smile back. "You happy to find out I'm not the spy?"

"I knew you weren't the spy." He squeezed her hand and then let it go.

Luci wanted to snatch his hand back, but she forced herself not to. "Hanna tried to get me away from the Red Building on the day of the attack." It hadn't seemed like anything important that day, but given the rest of Hanna's actions, Luci couldn't ignore it.

"What do you mean?" Ax asked.

"I was enjoying the sun in the quad. Then Hanna said we should get to class, but we still had a while before class was going to start so I said no. Then she tried to get me to go get a drink with her and I said no again. She was kind of insistent. But after I said no a third time, she took off. I kind of fell asleep and I'm not sure how much time passed after that—I don't think it was more than a few minutes—and then the attack started. Maybe Hanna had no idea what was about to happen, or maybe she was trying to get me out of the area. But if we're not friends, if I don't really know anything about her, I don't know why she would care." If Hanna was just using Luci as some sort of cover, she had no reason to care about her well-being.

"Knowing someone is not just knowing facts about them. You can like someone without any information," Ax said.

Was he really talking about Hanna? Luci wasn't brave enough to ask.

"She went into the Red Building and looked at a paper in the office where it looks like you guys fought. Then she burned it. That's all I saw."

Ax didn't have a response to that. They rocketed even higher, and it was another minute before something else changed in the cabin. Luci's arms rose up without her thought as her body suddenly went weightless. Her heartbeat kicked into overdrive at the sudden confirmation that they really were leaving Aorsa and headed for Kilrym or some other Apsyn stronghold.

Luci squeezed her eyes shut, as if that would somehow allow her to ignore what was really happening. This wasn't her first time in a spaceship. The last time she'd been on a ship they'd been rocketing away from Kilrym in the hope that they were finally safe from the Apsyns who had captured her and her fellow humans.

She pulled her arms in close to her body and hugged herself. It felt strange with the way gravity wasn't working. But Luci didn't want to think about why gravity wasn't working.

"No, no, no..." The protest escaped her mouth as she thought about exactly what had been done to her on Kilrym.

Ax unbuckled himself from where he'd strapped in and struggled towards her, movements difficult with the way gravity was working. He wrapped his arms around her, and that was even better than when they'd held hands. With his body pressed close, he was anchored to her.

But that didn't change the fact that they were heading back to Kilrym and to all of the dangers and evils that it contained.

And just as suddenly as the gravity disengaged, it reengaged, and all of Ax's weight came down on Luci, but she didn't let him pull away.

She was glad that the gravity drive had been engaged, or whatever it was that Hanna had done to make sure that the ship had its own kind of gravity.

Gravity was good. It made sense. Luci definitely preferred it.

And it calmed her mind a little, even though she was still fixated on the fact that they were headed straight to Kilrym and all that entailed.

"You're going to be okay," Ax promised as he clutched her close.

"You don't know that." He was strong. She knew that. He trained hard. But he was only one man. They were going to Apsyn territory. There were going to be plenty of soldiers. Plenty of people who could hurt them without a thought.

And it wasn't like Luci had a spark to defend herself. She didn't even have a weapon.

Not that she would know how to use one anyway.

In her desperation to feel safe, she almost offered to seal their Matched bond right then and there. If they did that, Luci would have magical electricity powers of her own, and she and Ax would be even stronger than they would be separately.

But that wasn't a decision to be made out of fear. And Luci wasn't sure what it would mean for them if they really took that step, so she clamped her mouth shut to keep from suggesting anything.

There was a small porthole on the wall nearest her, and when Luci looked outside, all she saw was black. Space. The ride between Aorsa and Kilrym didn't have to take long. But it was long enough for dread to build and build and build.

If Ax let go of her, she was going to be shaking.

She didn't want to shake. She didn't want to be afraid.

She wrapped her arms tight around him, but even that wasn't enough.

She needed more.

"Distract me," she begged.

"Do you want to hear a joke?" Ax asked lightly.

Despite herself, she laughed. "You know that's not what I mean."

She was afraid he would say no. Afraid that he would try and make some gentlemanly protestation about what she did or did not need. Luci knew what she wanted. She knew what she needed. And right now, she needed Ax and everything he could do to her. She ran her fingers down his back and up again, clutching him tight. "Please distract me." She would beg if she had to.

And with them pressed as close together as they were, she felt it when he gave into her request. His body shuddered, and then his mouth pressed hard against hers.

Yes. This was exactly what she needed.

1 2

NO FORCE in the universe could have stopped Ax from kissing Luci in that moment. It wasn't just the fear on her face. It was everything. She needed comfort, and he was the only one who could give it to her.

He'd be a monster to refuse.

But that wasn't the point. Not really. He couldn't resist her ever, and if he could find a way to keep her once they were safe back on Aorsa, he'd move all the stars to do it.

Not because she was his Match, but because she was Luci.

His mind was still ringing with the possibility of

125

the Match, even as he lost himself in her kiss, but that was a problem for another time. No, not a problem. It was a hope he couldn't even comprehend. He hadn't gone looking for his Match, and yet here she was. But if they bonded, it would change their lives in ways they couldn't begin to imagine.

For now he was going to put it out of his mind. Survive first, worry about the future later.

But even thoughts of long term survival paled in comparison to his plans for what to do to Luci next. Part of him wanted to rip her clothes off and have his way with her right now, to deepen the kiss with a feral intensity that would have her crying out for more. But Luci was still injured from her fight with Hanna, and he would not risk causing her even an instant of pain.

She reached for his shirt and jerked it up, but Ax placed a gentle hand on her wrist. "There's no rush."

"Isn't there?" Her eyes were still wild with fear, but lust was beginning to bleed in there, her cheeks flushed and breath coming faster. She was racing towards the end, but Ax wanted to show her how to savor the journey.

But to do that, he wasn't going to remind her of where they were and what was happening. It would be hours before they reached Kilrym, if that was where they were headed, but she wanted to forget why they had to pass the time, and he wasn't going to remind her. "No rush," he repeated, kissing her gently on her cheeks and then returning to her lips to savor her taste.

Luci's hands fell away and she let him lead the kiss, her tongue tangling with his and savoring the moment. He could spend a whole night like this, a whole lifetime, perhaps, but the current location left a lot to be desired.

He let one of his hands drift over the thin material of her pants at the juncture of her thighs, and Luci let out a surprised gasp at the contact. She caught on quick after a moment of confusion, spreading her legs and arching against him as he stroked her through her clothes.

It probably wouldn't be enough to get her off, but this wasn't just about the climax, it was about the moment and bringing her pleasure.

Something caused the ship to jolt and Luci froze, her entire body going tight with worry.

She didn't respond to his kisses, and Ax realized that this couldn't be solved completely with sex.

"Stay with me," he said, stroking her back and trying to ground her even as they hurtled through space. "You're with me."

"What if she finds us? She's going to kill us. Ax, I'm scared." It shuddered out of Luci and she hugged him.

"I won't let that happen. I will keep you safe.

Always." This wasn't his first time saying it, but this time Luci really seemed to understand.

"It's not supposed to be like this." It didn't sound like a rejection, even if her words were shaped like one.

"What isn't?" She'd spent the last weeks pretending every message they sent was nothing but sex and fun. And it was sexy and fun, but Ax couldn't hide his feelings anymore, and he wasn't going to pretend so Luci could push him away.

"You weren't supposed to be real." She kissed him, maybe to keep him from saying anything back.

Ax didn't know what he was supposed to say. Maybe a gentleman would have refused her kiss, but Ax couldn't refuse her anything, especially now. When she finally broke the kiss, all he said was, "I'm real and I'm yours."

Luci kissed him again, hard for a moment until she pressed against one of her cuts and gentled the kiss. He could feel her heart pour into it and knew this was a shift neither of them could come back from, not without heartbreak.

Ax dove right in. His heart could take the beating if it came to that, but he was hopeful enough to go headfirst and believe that all would end well.

He and Luci slid down to the floor of the cargo bay. It was hard and metallic and cold, but the heat of their bodies radiated out, and as their hands wandered and their lips clashed, they didn't care.

Luci shivered as Ax pushed her pants down, and he changed his plans. Maybe they would need to care a little bit about the temperature. He wasn't going to end this to go searching for a blanket.

He was pretty sure she would do her best to murder him if he did.

But they were keeping as many clothes on as they could.

Ax slid his own pants down and found Luci's entrance wet and hot and waiting for him. His own cock was iron hard and leaking in anticipation of delving into her tight heat.

He stretched her carefully, taking the time to savor every sound she made as he prepared her. Their eyes locked, and an awareness he'd never known before passed through them.

This wasn't just sex. Ax knew what just sex felt like, and while there was plenty of desperation and heat, his heart never felt like it might explode with want if he wasn't deep inside of her right then.

But with Luci that was all he knew.

"I'm ready. Please. Now," Luci demanded when she decided he was taking too long.

It startled a smile out of him. She knew what she wanted, and it was his pleasure to give it to her.

Always.

———

Luci had only wanted the distraction Ax could give her. That was what she told herself as she begged him to help her forget the terror of the moment. But the more he kissed and touched her, the more her heart melted.

She didn't just want his touch. She didn't just want a distraction.

She wanted all of him. And she could have him. If she was brave enough.

But Luci had already used up all her bravery, and she didn't know how to dig deeper to find any more. She'd made it this far on desperation and survival, and if she took a real chance, then Ax could hurt her more than any Apsyn ever could.

Still, she wanted to be brave. She wanted to give her heart and her body to him and trust that he wouldn't let her down. So many people had hurt her before. But Ax was different.

He could be hers.

"Please!" Ax's fingers were doing wicked things to her and her body was perched on the edge of release. She needed him inside her more than she needed her next breath.

And finally Ax gave her what she needed, his cock pushing into her slick entrance and fitting into her like they were made to be together.

And as a Match, weren't they? Sort of? That was a thought so scary that Luci had to push it to the very depths of her mind as she gave herself over to the sensation of Ax's body entering hers. This was what she needed, and all thoughts of the dangers they were heading straight into slipped away as she surrendered to sensation.

The metal of the ship's floor was hard against her back, but it was nothing compared to the pleasure of Ax's body pushing into hers. She kept her eyes open, watching as he moved, his face taking on an expression of concentration that looked almost painful.

They were both bruised and battered from the day, but this moment of joining was healing them in ways that no medicine ever could. Luci was connected to Ax not just in body, but in spirit as well, and for the first time in her life felt that this was truly what it was supposed to be like. She and Ax had fooled around before, and she wouldn't trade that pleasure for anything, but somehow this was more.

She gasped as he thrust deep and hit her just right, her body moving in time with his. He grinned at her response, and her heart flipped and then sped up even more as his thrusts got faster and faster.

Oh yes, he knew exactly what he was doing and she never wanted him to stop.

Luci couldn't keep quiet if she tried, but the ship

was already loud and they were far enough away from the cockpit that they didn't need to worry about Hanna hearing them. All thoughts of Hanna and danger were far away as her moans grew louder.

This was it. Exactly what she wanted and needed.

Ax sped up and Luci matched him, their bodies synchronized. There were no worries in this moment or thoughts of tomorrow, only the passion they shared with their bodies. She clung to him as she came, saying words she refused to remember as he brought her to the heights of pleasure.

They cuddled together as they caught their breath, sweat cooling on their bodies and making it chilly in the cargo bay. Ax ran hot and Luci stayed as close as she could, not bothering to tell herself that it was merely for warmth; she couldn't fool herself *that* much.

They didn't speak. Not for a long time. They lay together and gave each other a different kind of comfort, one that could only be given in silence.

Luci wanted to go home. But for the first time, she didn't imagine her home back on Earth. She imagined Human House and all the people she'd met in the last year. She imagined Aorsa.

She imagined Ax.

She knew she could never go back to Earth. Even if she could find a ship, it would take decades to get back, and Earth would have spun through more than a century since she'd last seen it. And given the state of the place when she left, she wasn't sure there even *was* an Earth to go home to.

A gasp tore out of her, followed swiftly by tears. Beside her, Ax jolted and looked at her, eyes wide.

Luci couldn't help but sputter out a teary laugh. "It's not you, I promise. It's not *this*." Of course crying right after sleeping with a guy couldn't be a balm to his ego.

He pulled her even closer. "We're going to get home, I promise."

"That's the thing, it really just hit me that I'm never going home. My parents are probably dead. Most of my friends too. And they'll never know what happened to me." Luci had been an only child and her parents had doted on her. At times she'd resented just how much they cared for her, and now thinking of that made her want to scream. She'd taken them for granted until it was too late to appreciate it.

Ax didn't try and tell her it was okay. He held her close and let her cry. She was so grateful that she was afraid she was going to cry harder about it.

Luci didn't know how much time passed with Ax silently holding her as she mourned for the life she'd never have. Slowly the tears subsided, leaving only the beginnings of a headache behind. Just what she needed on this terrible adventure.

She and Ax readjusted their clothes, putting back

on everything they'd removed and then laying back down together. And finally, peace settled over Luci. She didn't know what they'd be facing once they reached Kilrym. Everything could fall apart in a moment.

But she was with Ax, and she knew he'd lay down his life to keep her safe.

She wouldn't let that happen. She and Ax were going to find a way back to Aorsa. And she was going to seize her life with both hands and create something for herself.

"I can't make up for your loss. But if you want, I'll do what it takes to help you build something new. All you have to do is ask." She wasn't looking at him while he spoke, his body wrapped around hers like a big spoon. But she felt his breath tickle her hair and his lungs expand with every breath.

"When I'm ready to ask, you'll be the first to know."

13

Luci: Maybe I'll let you take me on that adventure.

LUCI SLEPT FOR A WHILE, and then she woke up and paced. And then she got kind of hungry. She and Ax managed to find a few protein bars hidden away in a med kit and ate them with the kind of gluttonous hunger that only came from starving. Not that they were actually starving, but they weren't going to take their chances.

It was almost shocking how bored she got while she waited in fear for them to arrive on Kilrym. But eventually the feel of the ship changed and they strapped in just in time for Hanna to approach the planet and bust through the atmosphere.

Oh. There was the panic.

It all rushed back to Luci, and if Ax wasn't right

there beside her, she had a feeling she would be screaming. But he was there, and she was able to hold that in.

They landed somewhere. That much was obvious when the ship came to a stop. Both she and Ax unclipped themselves from their seats and scouted around for a place to hide. The cargo bay wasn't big, and there weren't a lot of options. They ended up ducking behind a crate that wasn't quite large enough to shield both of them and waited.

Would Hanna come into the cargo bay? Were they about to be caught and handed over to the Apsyns?

Luci breathed in and out, trying to keep it even and to hold a panic attack at bay. She could freak out later. Besides, she'd already freaked out once. They didn't have the luxury of any more right now.

"If she comes for us, stay behind this crate. I'll handle it," said Ax with an easy kind of confidence that had to be a front.

"She could kill you." Luci didn't want to consider it, but Hanna was a mercenary or a spy or a soldier of some kind, and there was no way she was just going to let them go.

"I have my spark," said Ax. He didn't unfurl his wings, but Luci could feel the hair on her arms stand up with an awareness of electricity. "I can handle her."

"What about our Match?" She hadn't said anything about it earlier. It was almost too scary to contemplate. But she knew that Ax would be more powerful if they were to bond, and she would have wings of her own. Maybe they needed the power boost right now. She couldn't think beyond the next few minutes.

"We'll deal with that later," said Ax.

What was that supposed to mean? Later? There might not be a later. She was offering him power and herself. And here he was rejecting it. But Luci held those thoughts in. This was no time to start feeling bad about something she didn't even want in the first place.

She was pretty sure she didn't want it.

She thought she didn't want it.

Did she want it?

And it was thoughts like those that were going to cause her to hesitate and get both of them killed.

No. If Ax didn't think they needed to bond right now, then they didn't need to bond. She had to trust him. He was the one who had experience with battle and his spark.

Besides, she knew from her friends who were bonded that humans didn't magically know how to deal with a spark once they had it. Lena had been sent to some sort of remedial training camp to figure out how to use her powers. So maybe she would be more trouble than it was worth if she got powers right now.

And that made her feel worse.

The feeling bad about herself turned out to be an okay distraction while they sat in the cargo hold and waited to see what Hanna would do. They could hear her moving around through the door, and that was their sign to be as quiet as possible. If they could hear her, she could probably hear them.

Metal groaned, but it wasn't the interior door that led from the cockpit to the cargo hold. She was heading outside of the ship.

Luci let out a breath, and some of the tension in her spine began to dissipate, but she wasn't willing to think they were safe just yet. Hanna could be coming around the back to access the cargo hold that way.

She and Ax waited. And waited. And waited.

Five minutes or more must have passed; Luci didn't have a strong sense of time at that moment. There was only the anticipation.

Ax was the one who decided they needed to move.

"She's not coming back here," he declared and stood up.

Luci wanted to grab him back down. What if that was the moment that Hanna chose to open the door? But she didn't. That was her panic talking. They couldn't just stay in the cargo hold all day. They were on Kilrym, and they needed to make the most of it. They had to figure out what Hanna was trying to do and then find a way back home.

"Are we still locked in?" Their desperate attempt to escape on Aorsa clearly hadn't worked. And now Luci was wondering if they could get out of the cargo hold at all.

But Ax didn't seem concerned. "That was a safety measure to keep the bay doors closed during launch. We should be fine now." He crossed the cargo bay and looked out the small window beside the door. "I don't see anyone. Stay back there until the doors open. Only come when I call you."

Luci stayed. This was even scarier than waiting to see what Hanna would do. There could be an entire battalion of soldiers on the other side of that door ready with their sparks and their blasters and all the might of the Apsyn military. But there was only one way to find out.

Ax pressed the button to open the door and Luci held her breath.

It screeched open, and she winced at how loud it was. Didn't they oil those things? Anyone in a twelve mile radius would be able to hear it. She hoped Ax had taken cover, but she was crouched behind the crate and couldn't check.

She wished she was brave. She wished she was right there beside him facing whatever potential danger there was. But he had told her to hide, and he was the expert right now. So for now she would follow his lead.

It felt like forever but couldn't have been more than thirty seconds, and when the door was fully open, the screeching stopped.

Luci forced herself to stay put. Ax told her to wait, so she would wait. That was what she was supposed to do. She had to let him know that he could count on her.

But why was he taking so long? She was vibrating with the need to move, but she kept still. She had to do her part. She could do this. It was all right.

"We're clear," Ax said, summoning her from behind the crate. "We need to get out of here."

She couldn't agree more.

She approached the cargo bay and looked out. She saw buildings in the distance and vaguely recognized them. This was the capital city of Kilrym. She had been here before when she'd been held as a prisoner. She had hoped she would never be here again.

"We're going to find a safe place and you're going to wait there," Ax told her as he scanned the distance for any sort of trouble. "I'm going to find Hanna and see what she's up to. And then we're going to find a way out of here."

"I'm not staying put." Luci might have been

willing to follow his lead while waiting on the cargo ship, but she wasn't going to sit around like a sitting duck and wait for the Apsyn soldiers to find her.

"It's safer for you," Ax insisted.

"Not if they find me. I can't fight back. And you won't know where I've gone. I would rather die fighting them on my own terms at your side than be captured again." And she meant every word.

Ax studied her for several long seconds. "You follow my lead and do exactly as I say. Neither of us is going to get killed."

Ax knew he should have fought. Luci was no soldier, and she didn't have the kind of experience necessary for this mission. But he also knew that if he left her in some place, she would come chasing after him the second he turned his back. It wasn't about disrespect to him. It wasn't about him at all. She'd been held prisoner in this place and those memories had to be close to the surface.

He wanted to keep her safe however he could. But there was no safety here. And he would be lying if he said that he would feel better if they were separated. Even if it made no logical sense, if he saw her at his side, he could reassure himself that she was all right. Even if they were heading straight into danger.

But Luci wasn't stupid. She was willing to follow most orders. And she was observant. He could use somebody watching his back.

But it meant that he was going to take fewer risks. Because he might be willing to risk his own life, but he wouldn't risk hers. And if the choice was between getting both of them back to Aorsa or figuring out what Hanna was doing, he would be on the next flight out.

But he had a feeling that they couldn't leave this planet until they knew what was going on.

Just to check out that hunch, he led Luci around to the front of the ship and looked in the cockpit. It was bio-locked, presumably to Hanna, and there was no way to start up the ship and get them headed back home.

They would have to find another way off the planet. There were still shuttles that headed between Kilrym and Aorsa, though they were more heavily guarded than they were during peacetime. Sneaking onto one of them would be almost impossible, but it was an option. But their best bet was probably theft.

But they would deal with that later. Once they figured out what Hanna was doing and why she was stealing things from the University of Aorsa.

"Let's find our spy." He picked a path that seemed

most likely. Hanna was several minutes ahead of them and there wasn't an obvious trail. But there was a footpath that headed towards civilization, and that seemed like the logical option.

They weren't in a traditional space port. Hanna had landed in a large lot near several industrial buildings. He didn't see anyone else, but that didn't mean there wasn't security. If she really was working for the Apsyn military, there were going to be guards somewhere.

And then it occurred to him that maybe this wasn't a military mission at all. Maybe this was some sort of academic espionage. He hoped so. But given the current political situation, that didn't seem likely.

They did their best to be inconspicuous, and that meant walking around like nothing was strange. From a distance no one would be able to tell that Luci was a human, but if they got close they would be able to see the minor differences between their two species. On Aorsa it was no big deal. On Kilrym it could get them killed.

The Apsyns didn't see humans, or any non-Zulir, as people worthy of respect. They used humans as pets and slaves and science experiments. And perhaps the safest bet right then would have been to pretend that Luci was some mix of those three things and walk along as if that was their relationship.

But Ax would never ask that of her. Not after

everything she'd been through. She was standing on the precipice of her trauma, and he knew it wouldn't take much to push her over into a place she could never return from.

And luckily it wasn't necessary. After a few minutes of walking, they caught sight of Hanna just before she turned down a path that led closer to the buildings. He and Luci sped up to catch her, but as they moved, Luci tripped over her own feet and let out a curse.

At first Ax didn't think anything of it. Then he heard boots. Soldiers.

"Come on." He clamped a hand on Luci's arm and led her off the path towards a wooded area that would give them cover. They were just in time. Apsyn soldiers followed carrying large blasters, as well as a bonded pair with their enormous wings out, ready to fry anyone with an extremely powerful spark.

The soldiers looked around, but they didn't see anything.

Ax didn't even dare to breathe, and Luci was holding so still she might have been a statue. One of the soldiers looked at the woods, and Ax and Luci shrank further back into the foliage.

Don't come this way. Don't come this way. Don't come this way. It was a prayer and it wasn't answered.

Two of the soldiers headed off for the woods while the rest stayed on the main path.

He and Luci had to move.

The woods give them cover, but it was harder to move fast, especially since they couldn't disrupt any of the trees or make extra noise. It wasn't completely silent. There were animals on the planet, birds chirping and small furry creatures running around. But they didn't make as much noise as a human or a Zulir did.

Ax pushed Luci into the hollow of a tree and motioned for her to stay as quiet as she could. He moved the fallen branch in front of the opening to give her a bit more camouflage and then began to climb the tree as high as he could. It gave him an observation point, and if he had to fight, it was better to do it from the high ground.

He just hoped they didn't see Luci.

He looked back towards the buildings and saw Hanna enter one of them. Then his attention was drawn back to the forest. He couldn't really see the path with all of the leaves in front of him, but he tried. He was ready for the attack. He knew it had to be coming. He would fight with all he had.

But the minutes ticked by and the soldier didn't come.

A few minutes later, Ax saw all of the Apsyn soldiers, including the two who'd come into the woods, walking down the path and away from the building that Hanna had entered.

They must have been satisfied that no one was hiding in the woods.

That was lucky. Damn lucky. And Ax wouldn't be able to count on it forever.

But he scrambled down from the tree and got Luci out of her hidey hole.

"I saw where Hanna went. Let's go."

They were walking straight into danger, but they didn't have another choice.

14

Luci: I'm tougher than I look.

Ax: Believe me, I know.

BARK CLUNG to Luci's hair, but she was trying to ignore it. She wasn't eager to hide in another tree, and she hated to think of the potential for bugs crawling all over her. She shivered as she felt phantom legs skittering across her skin.

She was fine.

There were no bugs.

Please, she begged some unseen celestial power, let there be no bugs. She couldn't handle another thing going wrong.

Ax led her down the path and they snuck into the same building that Hanna had entered. It felt dangerous to do so, but Ax seemed to know what he was doing, and Luci had promised to follow his lead. So follow it she did, even as she bit back her doubts.

Hanna was waiting in the middle of the room, the large bag at her feet and her wings out, spark at the ready. She was holding herself like she didn't trust the people she was meeting. For a moment, Luci let herself believe that Hanna wasn't a spy, and this was all some big misunderstanding.

Then two Apsyn soldiers in military uniforms came into the room, and Hanna greeted them by name.

There was no innocent explanation for that.

"You retrieved it?" the first soldier asked. He had blue hair and wings that were bright red.

"Obviously," Hanna replied, letting her spark flare in a practiced flick over the bag. "Would I be here if I hadn't?"

Blue grunted. The other soldier, this one with black hair and green wings, just shook his head.

Blue reached for the bag but Hanna stepped in front of it. "I worked hard to get this. Where's my payment?"

Blue lunged for the bag, but Black held him back. "The credits have been transferred to your account," Black said, arm straining to keep his partner in place. "So once you hand over the package, our business is done."

Hanna studied Black and Blue for several

moments, brows drawn down in contemplation. "There was some interesting data to go along with this device. Illuminate me. What does it do?"

Blue lunged again, but it was useless against Black's hand. "That's none of your business," Black said.

At the same time Blue spoke, a fanatic lilt to his voice. "It'll stop the Synnrs. That's what matters."

Luci swallowed hard at the thought. Was this some sort of weapon? It didn't look big enough to be one. But maybe it was the building blocks of one. Was Hanna handing over the Death Star?

"Oh yeah?" Hanna asked, giving most of her attention to Blue, who was clearly the one who wanted to talk. "How's that?"

He stopped resisting in his partner's grip and rolled his shoulders. "Well, let's just say that Matches won't mean much to them any longer." Blue grinned evilly.

Hanna moved more fully in front of the bag. "What's that supposed to mean?" She didn't sound too happy about that.

Beside Luci, Ax held completely still, and if she hadn't known he was breathing, she might have thought he was a statue. She wanted to hear what the soldiers were going to say. Matching was sacred to the Zulir. But the Apsyns had been researching it for a long time to try and manipulate it. If they could do that, could do something to compromise Synnr Matches, they would have a weapon of untold destruction.

"Just give us the package and be on your way," Black said. He was done with the conversation. He flared his wings in warning.

Hanna let her spark expand until a dome covered the bag, protecting it. Luci had never seen anything like that before. Did Synnrs not use their sparks in that way? Or had she just not been paying attention?

"I have to insist," Hanna said. Her spark seemed to glow even brighter the longer they waited.

"If it's what was promised, we'll be able to break Matches," Black relented, frustration clear. "Our researchers are eager to apply this research."

"That's horrible." The word ripped out of Hanna. She couldn't have meant to say it out loud. But she sounded shaken. "You can't do that. You can't take someone's Match away."

"Those freaks want to make war. They should be ready to pay the price," said Blue.

"Take the credits back. I'm not giving this to you." Hanna moved back, taking the bag with her.

Both Black and Blue's wings flared. "We had an agreement," said Black. "Give us the bag and we let you walk away. If you make trouble, you're not getting out of here."

A smile bloomed on Hanna's face and she rolled

her shoulders. "I'm going to get out of here," she said. She flashed out with her spark, aiming first for Black and then for Blue and sending them flying back. She scooped up the bag and ran for the door, but the two soldiers recovered quickly.

Now would be the time for Luci and Ax to escape, but Ax didn't move. And since Luci was following his lead, she stayed just as still.

Of course they couldn't leave. They had to make sure that this technology didn't fall into Apsyn hands. If they could sever Matches, they could deplete the power of the Synnr military in a single strike. They couldn't do that.

And whatever Hanna's reasons were for fighting now, Luci was glad to see it. At least her friend, her *almost* friend, her fake friend, believed in something.

Hanna fought hard. She had some training, even Luci could see that, but against two soldiers it wasn't enough. Black and Blue were ruthless and eventually one of them pinned Hanna to the wall while the other approached and grabbed the bag.

Electricity crackled in Luci's hair, and she glanced to the side to see Ax summoning his spark.

He was going to get them caught. But maybe he could destroy technology. She didn't want to die right now, but some things were more important.

But Ax didn't engage with the soldiers. He cracked his spark loudly, and a large hunk of metal came crashing down from the ceiling of the warehouse. It was enough to startle the two soldiers into letting Hanna go. They whipped around, trying to see what had caused the commotion. And that was Ax and Luci's cue to leave.

Ax led her outside and Luci found out that her hands were shaking, something she hadn't realized when she was inside the building.

"I have to go back in and destroy that bag," said Ax. "I want you to hide."

Luci wanted to protest. They'd already had this conversation. But he was right. She needed to stay out of the line of fire and it would only be a few minutes.

"Promise me you'll come back." It was unfair to even ask, but how could she do otherwise?

Ax looked like he didn't want to say it. And he didn't. Instead he leaned forward and gave her a hard kiss before pulling away. "Find somewhere to hide. I will find you."

That was as much of a promise as she was going to get. Luci found somewhere to hide while Ax ran back into the building.

AX TRIED NOT to let the horror overtake him. A device that could sever Matched bonds. It was something that even the scariest children's story couldn't imagine. A Match was sacred. To even consider severing the bond was a torture deeper than anything dreamt in the depths of Braznon's bowels.

He had to destroy that technology before the Apsyns made it back to their headquarters. Once they had the data, they could re-create it. He couldn't let them do that.

Ax snuck back into the building and was surprised to find Hanna still fighting the Apsyns. She had had the perfect moment to escape when he provided the distraction, but judging by the scorch marks on the outside of the bag, she had stayed behind to try and destroy the technology herself.

He respected her a bit for that, even if she was the one responsible for putting them in the situation in the first place. But whether she was a spy or a mercenary, it was interesting to see that she had morals of her own.

Ax used his opportunity to send a flash of his own spark at the bag. This was his only attempted surprise and was sure to give away his position, but it was also his best chance to take out the technology.

But whatever bag Hanna had used, it seemed resistant to the electric power of a Zulir spark.

Punt. Ax would need to get closer and get into the contents of the bag if he was going to destroy it.

Hanna spared him a glance and grimaced when

she saw him. She must have recognized him from the campus. Her mouth opened for a moment, but she snapped it shut before she said anything. One of the soldiers sent another blinding blast of his spark their way.

But she didn't let that stop her. She kept flashing her spark at the two soldiers and she was good. A better marksman than Ax was, to be certain. He was much more likely to depend on powerful strikes, but she wielded her spark with a rapier's precision. She would be an amazing ally, if she wasn't an adversary.

One of the two soldiers, the one with blue hair, turned his attention to Ax while the one with black wings paid attention to Hanna. Ax sunk into the fight, returning blows of his spark and moving by instinct.

He and Blue were evenly matched. But Blue potentially had backup coming, and Ax could only rely on himself. It made him hungrier, more determined to win. But Ax had to get near the bag, and all Blue needed to do was keep him away from it. And he was good at his job.

Hanna started to get close and Ax took a chance to give her cover. He was almost certain he could rely on her for this one thing. She didn't want the Apsyns to get the technology either.

After a minute, the tenor of the battle changed. The bag ended up between the four of them and instead of fighting, Blue put up an impressive shield while Black darted forward for the bag. No matter how much power Ax or Hanna shot at them, they couldn't get through, and Black and Blue retreated with the prize in hand.

Ax looked at Hanna.

Hanna looked at Ax.

They could battle this out right here, right now. But that just meant that the Apsyn soldiers would get farther away. Ax chased after them while Hanna gave a shrug and retreated the other way. It didn't look like there was going to be any help from that quarter.

Ax had to find them.

He burst out of the warehouse just in time to see a vehicle speed away, and from the small glance he got through the windows, he was fairly certain it was Black and Blue.

He had to report this. He had to notify someone this was happening. If the Synnrs knew about it they could potentially defend against it. But until his report came in they were helpless.

He had to find Luci and they had to get home. The rest of it they could deal with later.

He wanted to call out for Luci and tell her it was safe, but that would just call more Apsyns down on them. That patrol was still somewhere, and he didn't want their attention.

He looked around, trying to spot the place Luci would hide.

But before he could find her, a feminine shriek reached his ears.

Luci.

He rushed in the direction of the sound and dove for cover when he saw what was happening.

The Apsyn soldiers had found her.

15

Luci: I had a nightmare. Distract me.

Ax: Want to talk about it?

Luci: I asked for distraction.

Ax: Sometimes talking is better.

Luci: You sure? (attached, a distracting picture)

Ax: I like distraction.

LUCI SCREAMED as the Apsyn soldier clamped a hand on her shoulder and jerked her out of her hiding place. She was sure she couldn't have been seen from the path, but apparently she was wrong. She struggled against him and managed to break free of his hold for a moment, but only for a moment.

There were two soldiers, two of the group that she and Ax had seen earlier. At least it wasn't all six of them.

But one of them flashed their spark at her and sent searing pain dancing along her nerves. Luci wished she had a weapon, a gun, a knife, anything that would allow her to fight back with some chance of winning.

But neither she nor Ax were armed. At least Ax had his spark.

But Ax wasn't there right now, so she needed to fight back by herself.

She dropped to the ground and rolled before they could shoot her with another blast of spark. That hurt, and she didn't want to get hit again. Her body remembered all the injuries Hanna had inflicted, even if the healing cream had done miracles to speed up the healing process. Still, it hurt.

Luci took off running, but she only made it a few paces before another blast of spark. It didn't hit her, but it was close, and she had to dive to the side of the path to avoid it.

The Apsyns marched after her. They weren't in any hurry, and that was scarier than being caught. They didn't see her as the kind of threat they had to run after. And they were right. Luci wasn't much of a threat. And she hated it.

If she got out of this, she was going to find a way to fight back. She was going to take self-defense classes or something. Something that would make an Apsyn regret ever touching her.

One of the soldiers kicked her side, and she had to roll over to try and protect herself. It didn't do much.

"What's a *human* doing here?" the Apsyn nearest to her asked his partner. He said human like it was a curse word, like she was less than a speck of dirt.

To an Apsyn, she was.

"Doesn't matter," said the other soldier. "Take care of it."

It. Her. She didn't like the sound of that.

Luci scrambled back before the Apsyn could do anything else to her, but she was running out of room to maneuver. She jumped up to her feet in the kind of move she could only pull off in the middle of a panic. She wasn't sure how she reared back and burst up like that, and she wasn't going to question it.

Luci darted for the trees. It was her best shot at some sort of cover. She zigged and she zagged as she ran, as if she was trying to escape an alligator. She vaguely remembered a YouTube video about how to escape beasts like that.

Apparently it also worked on Apsyns. At least on their spark. They didn't hit her as she dove for the trees.

But when she made it into the forest, she completely lost her bearings. There was no convenient path to walk along. It was all dense trees and old growth. This wasn't a hiking path or anything so tame, even though it was right off a road.

The soldiers chasing her had to slow, but they would see her before long. She didn't exactly blend in.

She didn't want to risk getting lost in the depths of the woods, but that was better than letting the Apsyns get her.

She chose a direction and started walking. She tried to be as quiet as possible and winced every time she broke a branch or crunched a leaf underfoot. Hopefully the Apsyns wouldn't realize that was her.

But eventually they would call for backup. And once they did, she was toast.

Where was Ax? Why wasn't he here? Had Hanna done something to him?

She hoped not. But Ax had to handle himself. And Luci had to survive until he could find her.

Branches cracked behind her with a sizzle of electricity. The Apsyns were close and they could bring down the trees with the power of their magic. Luci didn't want to see that. And she didn't want to get crushed by branches. She picked up her pace and hoped she was going in the right direction.

One turn and then another and then another, and somehow she found herself right back on the walking path and near the warehouse where she'd escaped from in the first place.

She came face-to-face with Ax, who looked at her with the kind of shock that only came from watching someone you thought was dead miraculously recover. Then his eyes got even wider.

"Drop. Now." She didn't know why he was yelling, but the command in his voice was enough to make her hit the ground.

Ax let off a spectacular burst of his spark and she heard two thuds as bodies hit the ground.

She tried to look over behind her where the soldiers were coming from, but Ax put a hand on her shoulder. "Stay here," he told her. "Don't look."

In her heart, she understood what he was saying. Why he didn't want her to look back. If those soldiers reported back to their commander, then they were going to turn Luci and Ax in. They couldn't survive this encounter. If they didn't show back up, there was a chance that their people would think they had just deserted. That was better than the other option.

She did not watch Ax as he finished off the two soldiers. He had asked her to look away. He was trying to spare her that nightmare. So she would honor the request.

Her adrenaline was making her shaky and she wanted to find a place to hide. She wanted to go home and wanted this whole nightmare to be over.

But every time she thought that, things just got worse.

It was a few minutes later when Ax came back. Luci scrambled up to her feet.

"We need to go find a place to hide," said Ax. "I don't know when their friends will be coming back."

"Should we try and hide the bodies?" She felt sick asking it. But Luci had to fall back on the need for survival. She could freak out more later.

"I dragged them into the foliage. We don't have time to bury them. Let's go."

Luci didn't look back over her shoulder and try and grab a glimpse of the dead soldiers. They were dead. She was alive. That was war.

But this war could not be over soon enough.

Ax HAD to keep his cool. He could see that Luci was hanging on by a thread, and if she knew how he really felt, that might send her off into a panic, and neither of them could afford that.

He'd hidden the bodies well enough that he didn't think they would be found for a couple of days. Not if they were lucky.

Of course, his relationship to luck in the past day and a half wasn't exactly good. But they needed to do something. They couldn't let the Apsyns keep that device that could potentially break all Synnr Matches. It wouldn't be long before they transported it to their headquarters. So he had to act fast.

And he was going to need Luci's help.

They found a burned out little building that looked like a strong wind could push it over, but it was far enough out of the way that Ax doubted it was on the main patrol path of the soldiers in the area. He and Luci snuck inside and looked around. It wasn't too bad as far as burned out husks of old buildings went. It would provide them shelter for the night.

And hopefully it would give Luci the kind of protection that whatever hiding space she had found earlier hadn't.

"You should stay here. I need to go get that bag back. The Apsyns can't have it. And there's a good chance Hanna is looking for us too. She must have put you on that ship for a reason." Ax didn't know how he was going to assault four soldiers by himself, but he had to do it. Hanna was nowhere to be seen, and Luci didn't have battle experience or a weapon. He was the soldier here. He had to do this alone. Hanna may have allied with him in the moment, but he didn't trust her. There was no good reason to bring a human to Kilrym.

"What do you mean?" asked Luci. She sank to the ground and pulled her legs in close, huddling into a ball as if she were freezing.

Ax wished he had a blanket or something to offer her. All he had was himself. He got close and wrapped an arm around her, trying to share his body heat as best he could.

"Hanna and I fought them, but they got the device. They're going to send it on to their headquarters. I have to get it back. Or destroy it. Either way works. But they can't have it." He and Luci weren't bonded, but the awareness of their Match lingered at the periphery of his mind. He couldn't imagine the kind of turmoil a person would go through if their Match was ripped away from them. He couldn't let his people suffer.

"If you go alone, you're going to die." Luci said it with certainty.

And it was a fear that lived in the back of Ax's mind. But he didn't have another choice. "If that piece of tech works, it's a guarantee that they'll win the war. They will destroy life as we know it in the Synnr kingdom. I have to stop them." He had a duty as a Synnr and a soldier.

He expected Luci to fight some more. He didn't expect her to nod in agreement. "I thought you would say that. I think we should seal the bond."

His first response was to deny it, but he clamped back the words. He didn't want Luci to think she was being rejected. He would never reject her. But this wasn't a decision that could be made rashly. Once they sealed the bond, they would be stuck together for the rest of their lives. It was the kind of fate that Ax dreamed of when it came to Luci, but he wouldn't force her into it.

And he couldn't let her make a decision based on fear.

"We should think about it before we do anything," he cautioned. He wanted it. He wanted Luci at his side more than anything. But he feared she would come to regret this, and he couldn't let her do that.

But Luci had her own thoughts on the matter. "If I had a spark, I could have fought back against those soldiers better. They almost killed me. They almost captured me, more importantly. We don't have a blaster. We don't have anything except your spark. And if we bond, then I will have a spark, and we'll both be stronger than you are right now." She knew what she was talking about. A Matched and bonded Zulir pair were stronger than a single Zulir warrior.

The Match amplified each person's spark and made them about twice as powerful as a single Zulir. Of course, humans didn't know how to use their sparks, and it took some time to train it. There was no guarantee that Luci would have the power even if they bonded. But Ax would be twice as powerful. Perhaps powerful enough to take on four trained soldiers.

"I don't want to force you into something like this.

We are Matched. That's not going to go away. But you shouldn't feel like this is something you have to do."

"Isn't it?" she shot back. "We need power. We need a weapon. There are at least four soldiers out there and Hanna and a planet full of Apsyns who are likely to kill us or turn us in if they find us. This is something we need to do."

"This won't go away when we get back to Aorsa. We will still be bonded. Is that something you can handle?" She didn't want a long-term relationship, or at least that's what she'd been saying before they left Aorsa. Would this change things? Or would it just make them worse?

"I know how it works," Luci insisted. "And as for us… If it had to be anyone, I'm glad it's you." Her eyes were wide and honest as she said it, chest heaving. He believed her.

Not exactly a declaration of love or eternal devotion, but Ax couldn't help the satisfaction that suffused him. She wanted him. Even if she wasn't sure how or why or what would end up between them, she wanted him.

"Let's do it." She was right. He needed the power. And if they were Matched, they had a fighting chance. "Do you know how?" he asked.

"Not exactly," Luci admitted.

This part Ax knew. All Zulir did. "What you're going to do is concentrate and follow the feeling of the Match until you feel my power. You're going to grab it and use it. And I'm gonna do the same for yours. That seals the bond." At least theoretically. Obviously Ax had never actually done this. But it wasn't supposed to be difficult.

Luci gave him a jerky nod and then squeezed her eyes shut.

Ax waited to see what she did. He wasn't sure if he was supposed to be able to feel her reaching for his power or if it was something that was just going to happen. But a moment later, he felt like he'd been punched in the chest, and he saw sparks dancing on Luci's fingers.

Her eyes got wide and she let out a surprised bark of laughter. "I did it!"

He wanted to kiss her. But they were in the middle of their bonding and he needed to do his part. Ax sank into his power and followed it until he could feel the bond between himself and Luci. He reached deep, deeper into his own power than he had ever gone, and beyond it until he had his hands around the kind of power he'd never felt before. It wasn't Zulir, wasn't Synnr. It was human. It was Luci.

He didn't want to take too much. He didn't want her to feel a moment of pain. He pinched off a bit of her power and pulled it back into himself, and when he opened his eyes, energy crackled in his palm.

The bond settled into place between them, solid and permanent and everything he'd ever wanted.

He had to find a way to survive the coming battle. Because he wanted to feel this way forever.

Luci: What's it like to have magic powers?
   Ax: What?
   Luci: Um… forget I asked.

LUCI HAD MAGIC POWERS. Holy crap. She was a freaking superhero.

She could feel the electricity buzzing in her veins, and this time it wasn't any sort of metaphor. She had real powers. She had seen the evidence in her own hand.

And she was bonded to Ax.

If she thought about that too much, she would go crazy. Not that the superpowers made her feel any less crazy. It was all completely unbelievable. Then again, her entire life was unbelievable. Every moment since she had been nabbed from Earth and awoken on a planet so far away that no one back home even knew it existed.

"How do you feel?" Ax asked, placing his hand over hers and linking their fingers together.

She liked that. A lot. She could feel the magic between them gather in their joined hands. Or maybe that was just the warmth of his skin. She still had to figure these things out.

"I feel like I could kick some Apsyn ass." That was the right answer. It had to be. Luci wanted to rain destruction and hellfire down on these people. And now she had the power to do it.

Ax smiled. "Not just yet. Let's see what you can do." He looked around the room and then gave a small shake of his head before standing up and tugging her up beside him. "Let's go find a target."

They left the shelter of their building. Probably for the best. Luci had heard that new powers could be a bit volatile, and she didn't want to bring the building down on top of them. Ax took her into the forest, and while there had been no path for her to follow, he didn't seem to have the same problem. He stepped with a confident surety that made her jealous. But she just copied his steps and hoped it was good enough.

They came to a small clearing deep into the

woods, and Ax pointed at a large tree trunk about twenty feet away. "Hit it with your spark. Let's see what you can do."

Easy enough. If Luci had a baseball or something, she could probably throw it and hit the tree. So why would her spark be any different? But now that they were in the forest, she felt like she was being tested, and suddenly nerves sprouted. She had never been the best at taking tests. Performance anxiety. It was a real thing. But this was easy. All she had to do was prove that she could use her powers. She could feel them. There was that electricity deep inside her that hadn't been there before. Brand new and all hers.

All hers and Ax's. It felt like him. A little bit. She was going to be carrying a piece of him around for the rest of her life. And while that might have freaked her out before, now it comforted her. She didn't mind having Ax at her side.

Luci looked at the tree and tried to gather up her power. It didn't feel like much. Or rather, it felt like when she was a little kid and she and her friends decided to play superheroes.

Ridiculous.

She wasn't playing superheroes now. Now she was going to use her powers for real.

With no other idea, she concentrated on centering her power in her hand and wrenched her arm forward, flicking her wrist as if she actually was throwing a baseball.

Nothing happened. There was no spark. No lightning. Not even a puff of smoke.

Luci glared at her hand. And then her gaze snapped up to Ax and she pointed at him preemptively. "Let me figure this out." She didn't need his advice. Or maybe she did. But she wanted to see if she could do it on her own first.

The Apsyns were out there somewhere. If they caught them, they would capture or kill them. And now Luci had a way to fight back. She had to figure out what she was doing.

The baseball throw didn't work. What about lightning hands? She held her hands in front of her, fingers splayed, and imagined lightning shooting out of her fingertips. It worked in the movies.

It did *not* work in a forest on Kilrym.

She held up her hand, palm out to ward off Ax's advice one more time. Maybe it wasn't the action. She had to get the power first. She closed her eyes and took several deep breaths, in and out and in and out. She reached for her power. It was right there. She needed it in her hands.

Did she, though?

She needed the power in the tree. Not in her hands. So instead of focusing on bringing the power to the surface of her own body, she thought of directing it towards the tree in a blinding crack.

Something snapped against her chest and she heard a branch crack.

Smoke sizzled in the air, and Luci opened her eyes to see a giant crack formed in the base of the tree.

"Yes!" Ax pumped a fist in the air before gathering her up in his arms and swinging her around. "You did it."

"I did it!" Luci wanted to dance in celebration, but Ax was holding her too tight. Never mind dancing. This was better. She leaned in and kissed him, but it was quick. They didn't have time for much more. "Satisfied? I'm ready to take on an Apsyn army."

He kissed her. "They should fear you. But let's try a little bit more."

Luci was ready to fight battles, but she had to admit that Ax had a point. She turned back to the tree and tried again. She tried to do exactly the same thing, focusing on her power and sending it toward her target rather than summoning it into herself.

Nothing happened.

Damn it.

She tried again, even harder.

Still nothing.

Luci punched towards the tree and a crack of spark came out of her.

Okay. That was little different. But it still worked. She just needed to figure out how to make her powers work more than one third of the time.

"Are you ready for some advice?" Ax asked. He was watching her with a calculating look. Clearly he'd been biting his tongue for some time.

But she had tried it on her own. She had done it successfully on her own. And now maybe he could give her some pointers on how to make it even more successful.

"Give me what you got."

Ax came up to her and grabbed onto her arms. He guided her through the motions of summoning her spark and sending it shooting out of her right towards the tree. Even with his help it was still hard, but he explained the fundamentals of getting power and using it. These were things that the youngest Zulir children understood. But Luci tried not to get hung up on that. She was doing it. Things were going well. She had powers and she could use them.

Sometimes.

But they were taking a lot of time, and every minute they spent practicing was a minute that the Apsyn soldiers could be using to take the tech back to their headquarters.

"I'm not going to get perfect at this," she told Ax. She would train for hours if that was what it took, but they didn't have hours to wait.

He didn't fight her. Instead, he looked resigned. "Don't use your spark unless you have no other choice."

Okay, so maybe she wasn't as good at her powers as she thought.

But they were going to get this done. They had tech to steal.

AX WAS PROUD OF LUCI. She had an aptitude with her spark that was almost unheard of in a human. At least when it came to first using it. He had heard what the other humans from her group who had bonded with Synnrs went through. It could be excruciating to figure out how to use a new spark.

And Luci had figured it out in a matter of minutes. And she had the kind of power that some Synnrs would envy.

But she still lacked control. He tried to keep any worry off his face. He didn't want her discouraged. She could do something, and that was better than nothing. It would have to be enough.

He could feel his own powerful spark in his veins. Much stronger than he expected. If he wasn't careful he could kill somebody with his new power.

The lives he had already taken weighed heavily on his conscience. This was war. That was what happened. He hadn't hesitated in the moment, and he wouldn't hesitate in the future. But he would remember what it felt like to watch the life drain out of another person's eyes until his dying day.

As far as they knew, there were four more Apsyn soldiers lurking around somewhere. Whether or not they had called for backup after the other two soldiers disappeared would be the question. Soldiers had a habit of disappearing on Kilrym. Normally just for a night of revelry in the city or to take a much-needed break. There were not harsh penalties for Apsyn deserters.

So hopefully that was where the Apsyn thoughts would lie.

"We need a distraction," Ax said. Facing four soldiers head on could easily get them killed, and he didn't want to risk it. Not if there was another way.

"Fire?" Luci asked, catching the way he was thinking.

He smiled. "Fire."

They had the choice of empty warehouses and chose the one farthest from the building they were staying in to hopefully hide their presence. Ax used his spark to start a fire and waited to make sure that it spread, smoke billowing high in the air.

They headed towards the guard station and found a guard vehicle on their way. Ax set that ablaze as well. If they didn't notice the warehouse, the guard vehicle was sure to have an alarm that would alert them to the issue.

He and Luci hid. They had to see what the guards would do.

And the guards came running.

They wouldn't have much time, but they would take what they could get.

In the dash to deal with the car, the guards had left the door to the guard station opened. Incompetent. A Synnr officer would have whipped Ax for something so negligent.

He thanked the lax Apsyn training.

"Look around. See if you can find the bag," he told Luci. The room was small. The guards were staying in a house beside one of the larger warehouses. There were only two rooms, a command station and a bunk room. There were bags in the bunk room, but they only contained the guards' clothing and personal items. Ax didn't see the bag that Hanna had brought to them.

He went back to the command center, where Luci was on her hands and knees looking in every nook and cranny to see where they could find the bag.

"Shit," she said in one of those strange Earth curses.

"What is it?" he asked.

"A safe." She scrambled back onto her feet and nodded to a large dark box under the desk.

Ax took her place and attempted a few override codes on the control pad. None of them did anything.

Braznon's bowels. The bag had to be in there. These Apsyns were incompetent, but they would have to be completely stupid not to lock up the piece of tech that Hanna had brought them. Ax tried picking up the safe, but it was too heavy to shift by himself, and while he and Luci might have been able to move it, he didn't know if they'd be able to get away while carrying it.

But it was still here. They hadn't managed to take it back to headquarters yet. That was something.

"Hey, come look at this," said Luci.

Ax got to his feet, grateful to no longer be kneeling on the hard floor. "What?"

She had a piece of paper in her hands and handed it over to him. Ax read it.

A schedule. Good.

"Two days," he said as he figured out the date on Kilrym.

"Two days," Luci agreed.

The soldiers were scheduled to head out in two days' time to deliver the device to their headquarters. For some reason they weren't supposed to leave before then.

"They'll have to take it out of the safe to put it in a vehicle, won't they?" Luci asked.

Ax wasn't certain about that. But the device would be mobile. They had to be able to carry it somehow. And a convoy wasn't coming for it.

Maybe it wasn't as important as he was worried about.

Maybe the tech was only in its infancy. If an Apsyn deserter had brought something like this to Synnr territory, an entire battalion would be there to protect it. Not just a handful of soldiers.

He might have been risking his and Luci's lives for something inconsequential.

But maybe it was so hazardous, so confidential that the Apsyns didn't want to risk anyone else finding out about it before it was in their headquarters.

Ax didn't know if he believed that. But they needed to either get it back or destroy it.

"Do you think you can destroy the safe?" Luci asked. Her thoughts were taking a very similar turn to his.

Ax got back down on his knees and felt the middle of the safe. Then he shook his head. "No. Safes like these are rated to withstand a Zulir's spark. If I damage it, they will know that we were here."

And they were running out of time. Those fires wouldn't take long to deal with.

"We come back in two days. We hit them when they transport the device. It's our only shot."

Luci nodded, face grim. They were going to complete this mission. And then they were going to go home. Ax would do whatever it took to make sure that happened.

$$17$$

Luci: Can I come over later?
Ax: Anytime.

LUCI WATCHED Ax setting up defenses in their tiny shelter. It wasn't much. The roof—the parts that were intact, at least—didn't look likely to fall in on them, but that was her only hope. The place was covered in dirt and debris, and she was pretty sure creepy crawly animals had made a nest in one of the corners.

Home sweet home.

But she was with Ax, and that almost made it worth it.

He'd taken off his shirt to let it hang off of what once might have been a chair. The air was warm enough that they didn't need to worry about a chill, and Luci appreciated the view. Muscles worked under taut skin, skin she'd touched every inch of.

And she wanted more.

Heat pooled low in her. It should have been impossible to feel this much want now, when they were in so much danger, but her emotions were all scrambled together. She always wanted when she was with Ax. He awakened things in her that she'd never even thought to crave.

He set a final alarm consisting of some string he'd found tied across the entrance like a trip wire and then came back to where she was sitting. He reached for his shirt, but Luci stopped him.

"Keep it off." She liked looking at him too much to let him hide behind a dirty shirt.

Ax's grin was carnal. "Yeah? Convince me." His spark was dancing in his eyes along with the challenge. She could see it all.

No, not just see, she could *feel* it in her veins. Their power was merged together, churning in both of them and getting stronger by the minute. Luci felt a burst of confidence and sent a jolt of her spark in Ax's direction. She wasn't even close to hitting him, but that wasn't the point. "There's more where that came from," she promised.

He laughed, hand still poised over his shirt. "You know your spark can't hurt me."

So that was how he wanted to play it. Luci

narrowed her eyes and summoned her spark again, this time aiming right for him. He absorbed the power and seemed to glow for a minute with the excess before it rushed back down their bond and into her.

Luci shivered, her nipples hardening with want. If Ax touched her right now, she'd be wet. God, she wanted him.

"You're playing a dangerous game," he warned.

She smiled. "Good."

Ax was on her in an instant, mouth crushed against hers as her legs went around his hips. She felt the iron hard length of him through his pants and wanted more.

But he took his time with the kiss, torturing her mouth with sweet caresses of his tongue and lips, dazzling her and making her forget the danger of the moment.

It all drifted away in the feel of Ax. She let herself get lost as she ran her hands over his skin, sighing against him and letting his body shield hers from all the danger that surrounded them. There was no safety on Kilrym. This would be the place her nightmares were made of for the rest of her life.

But Ax protected her from it as much as she could be protected.

He peeled her shirt off, careful not to rip it. They had to be cautious; they had no other clothes to wear and she didn't want to fight the Apsyns in a ripped top. But the heat in her body wanted her to throw caution to the wind and let Ax rip away.

He was keeping a more level head than she was.

Time for that to change.

They paused their kissing just for long enough to lose the rest of their clothes. Luci's throat rumbled with a growl—an actual *growl*—as Ax took the time to pile everything on the chair before coming back to her.

"You'll thank me later," he murmured against her.

Now was not the time to get caught up on later. Luci wrapped her fingers around his length and stroked him, deep satisfaction suffusing her at his masculine groan of pleasure. She made him make these noises, and it was a kind of power she'd never dreamed of. How had she ever imagined she could play with this man and let him go?

No, she was keeping him. For good.

She stroked him and watched as his expression surrendered to the pleasure. She could bring him over like this, watch him explode with lust and satisfaction. But they both needed more right now. This coupling was about both of them.

And when Ax grabbed her wrist and tugged her away from his cock, she let him. She was ready for him when his own fingers rubbed against her entrance and dove in, stretching her tight heat.

She wanted him fast and hard, without any of the preamble, but Ax took his time. This, too, was a torture. Her mate tortured her with pleasure, and Luci was finding out she was a very specific kind of masochist.

Then he was there, the blunt head of his cock entering her and stretching her even more. It was a tight fit, and Luci groaned as he pushed in, inch by inch, loving the play of her muscles as her body moved to accommodate him.

And as their bodies joined, she could feel their sparks dancing together in their veins, the reminder of the bond they would forever share. This was what it meant to be connected to another person, Luci knew, to find a perfect match and never let go.

There was a word for it. Something she should say. But her brain wasn't even brave enough to think it. And as she and Ax began to move, conscious thought was subsumed into visceral feeling and she gave herself over to it, moaning as Ax moved just *right*.

That was it.

That was perfect.

Her body began to convulse just as his cock started to vibrate in that particularly Zulir way, bringing her over the edge as he spilled into her, both of them breathing heavily, hearts in synch.

"They're going to kill us." That shouldn't have

been the first thing out of her mouth as they cuddled together, sweat cooling in the warm air.

"I'll keep you safe," he promised.

Luci could feel her spark and Ax's confidence. He believed that, she was sure.

But they were stuck on the wrong planet and surrounded by hostile forces. She snuggled closer to her mate. If they didn't have much time left, she wanted to make every minute count.

18

Luci: If we were back on Earth and I had powers, I would get in so much trouble.

Ax: Powers?

Luci: You know, shooting lightning from my fingertips.

Ax: Do you want them?

Luci: It would be kind of cool.

LUCI HAD a day to figure out how to make her powers work consistently. That wasn't daunting at all. Who was she kidding? She was shaking just thinking about it. She could feel her spark. She knew the power lived within her. But actually making her powers work on command was another story entirely.

She and Ax had found another tree for her to

practice on. They were far enough away from where they knew the Apsyn soldiers were patrolling that they were unlikely to be found. If Luci couldn't hit a tree at twenty paces, how was she going to hit a moving soldier?

"You can do this," Ax assured her. "You did it yesterday. Just focus and let your powers go."

Just focus. He made it sound easy. It wasn't. Luci wanted to complain. But she wasn't a child, and complaining would get her nowhere.

"Focus. Focus." Maybe if she said it out loud, that would actually help.

Nope. She still wasn't sure how to get her powers from inside of her body and into the tree.

She centered herself, breathing in and out like she was in a yoga class. She knew that the Apsyn soldiers wouldn't give her time to actually think about what she was doing, but that would be a problem for another day. She could work on speeding up using her powers once she actually had an idea of how to use them in the first place.

She shot both her hands forward like she was some sort of cartoon character and jumped back in surprise when there was an actual crack and her spark hit the tree.

Beside her, Ax grinned. "Now do it again."

But Luci was a little shaken up from the power

actually working. "I did it. Can't we celebrate that first?"

He gave her a searing kiss, one Luci felt all the way down to her toes. She leaned back in when Ax pulled away, but he was determined to get to work.

"Good job," Ax told her. "Now do it again."

She stuck her tongue out at him. She couldn't resist. She tried again. The same focus, the same move, the same everything. But the powers didn't come. What the hell? She breathed slowly. She was going too fast. She could do this.

She thrust her hands forward and felt the power leave her body.

Another success.

After that, Ax gave her pointers. They managed to get it so she was hitting the tree seven times out of ten, which was better than nothing, and she was able to eventually get her speed down so that she only took a few seconds to focus rather than the better part of a minute. She wouldn't be able to face a soldier head-to-head in some kind of spark-fueled duel, but maybe she could be backup.

Maybe this would work.

"I want to see what you're working with," she told Ax, confident now that she'd successfully managed a few tries.

"You have definitely seen what I'm working

with," Ax teased, and there was a whole world of promise behind his words.

Luci hated the blush she felt bloom on her cheeks, but she did her best to ignore it anyway. "Your spark, show it to me."

He put her to shame. Of course he did. He'd had a lifetime of working with his magic. Luci was working on about a day. She tried to remind herself of that. Tried to stay proud of what she could do. But it was difficult.

She had seen Ax use his spark before, and now it was at least twice as big as it had been before they bonded. That was good. They would need the power.

"Try and hit me," Ax said.

"What?" Last night it had been a tease, but today it felt much more serious.

"We are bonded," Ax reminded her. "Your power recognizes my power. You can't hurt me with it. I can't hurt you with mine. But you need to try and hit a person. I'm a much smaller target than that tree."

"Hit me first," she said. She needed the reminder that they couldn't hurt one another, and she needed to know what it felt like to get hit.

Ax leveled a look at her. He wasn't pleased. But he didn't hesitate, summoning a flash of spark in his hand and tossing it her way. It hit her in the center of her chest, and he was right. It did not hurt.

It sort of tickled.

Ax seemed to be able to regulate his, but she wasn't anywhere near that skilled. So she hoped he was right when he said that she couldn't hurt him, because right now she was trying for brute force.

She concentrated for a moment and then sent a blast of her spark his way.

He grunted as he absorbed the power and fell back a step.

"You just about kicked me in the chest," he said.

"Did it hurt?" She wanted to rush over and check, but she forced herself to stay still. Ax would tell her if he needed help.

He shook his head. "I'm fine. You might have bruised me. But I'll live."

He'd better. They shot their sparks back and forth for a while before Ax made it even more difficult, dodging out of the way while Luci concentrated on summoning her own powers.

Bastard. She needed to think before she summoned her power, but if he was moving all over the place, she couldn't figure out where to send it.

She got one lucky strike in by guessing where he was going to be, but the rest of her shots went wide. If she was lucky, she should be able to distract the Apsyns, but that wasn't much help.

"You need to be faster," Ax told her.

"No shit." She was getting frustrated. This training session had started out so well, but had quickly soured. Sure, she could hit a stationary target at twenty paces, but she couldn't hit a person. And it was even worse because she knew Ax was going easy on her.

The Apsyns would be doing everything they could to fire back at her, to hurt her.

"We can take a break," Ax offered.

"No. Again." Luci wanted to drill until she got this. She knew she wouldn't be much help, but she wanted to give Ax her best. They didn't have a lot of time to train, but she wanted to use every minute.

She lost track of time as they shot their powers back and forth. But eventually she was ready to fall over in exhaustion. Using a spark took energy, and they'd been going at it for hours.

She finally took a seat on the ground, ready to rest. Ax offered her an energy bar that he had scavenged from the building they were staying in. She ate gratefully. They didn't have much food, but they had enough for a couple of days. She hoped that was all they needed.

"You're doing well," Ax assured her. "No one gets it perfect the first try."

"Yeah, but the stakes aren't so high for kids practicing their powers."

He put an arm around her and held her close as she ate the energy bar. There was not much else he could say to reassure her. They were heading into battle with no weapons except the power that they carried inside of themselves. If they weren't good enough, they were going to die. And if they failed in this mission, they might be dooming all of the Synnrs back home.

It was a heavy weight on Luci's chest. One that wouldn't go away. But she wasn't going to fail Ax. She would die trying to succeed.

AX COULD TELL that Luci was getting more frustrated. He called an end to their training. They'd spent the entire morning trying to get her powers under some sort of control. No matter how much he praised her, he knew that she did not see her successes, only her failures.

Ax didn't know what to say to get her to believe that she was actually doing well. He would have to adjust the battle plan to make sure that she was as far away from the soldiers as possible. But she would be able to offer him some kind of backup, of that he was certain.

But they needed a better idea of what they were up against.

After a quick rest, he and Luci headed back toward the building where the guards were stationed and set up an observation post in the woods. It was risky to stay there, but they needed to be able to see what was going on.

There were still just the four guards. Apparently they weren't too concerned about their missing comrades.

Interesting.

Ax noted that, but even if more guards had shown up, there wasn't anything he could do about it. He considered whether or not it would be best to try and lure more of the guards away. Eventually he decided against it. There was too much of a chance that they would call for backup.

He wasn't putting Luci in that situation when they knew that the guards were going to move in two days. Less than that now. Tomorrow.

"Is soldiering work always this exciting?" Luci asked, voice dripping with sarcasm.

They had been sitting in the woods for a couple of hours, and nothing was happening. The guards had patrolled once, and he and Luci had shrunk back into the foliage and held their breath to make sure they weren't spotted. That was it.

"Sometimes," Ax admitted. Being a soldier was running from one boring post to another with brief bits of harrowing excitement that got Ax's blood pumping in the moment, but made him wish they never happened as soon as they were over. He didn't tell that part to Luci. She would figure it out for herself soon enough.

"What are you thinking about?" she asked after more silent observation.

"Exit strategies." He was studying the guards' building as well as he could without any schematics. They needed a way to get out after stealing the tech. He already knew that he would have to kill the four soldiers if they were going to get away. That was their only chance. But they would have to get off the planet quickly. Two disappeared soldiers could easily be deserters. But an entire team of six?

No. The Apsyns would know something was up.

There was an abandoned vehicle outside the building where they were staying, and luckily, it functioned. Ax hoped it would be good enough to get them somewhere where they might be able to find a ride off the planet.

He had contacts in the city of Vanen, and he hoped they were still around and would be able to get a message to the Synnrs for him.

It all hung on hopes and fragile bonds. He didn't tell that to Luci. He didn't want her worrying yet.

One threat at a time.

The hair on the back of Ax's neck prickled and he looked around.

The soldiers weren't coming. The forest was quiet, but not eerily so. Everything seemed normal.

But he felt like he was being watched.

He wanted to leave the station to go investigate, but he wasn't going to abandon Luci.

Was there another soldier unaccounted for?

What about Hanna? He didn't know where that woman went or what her plans were. She had to be in just as much trouble as he and Luci were. She had fought the Apsyn military and run away. They weren't going to look too kindly on her.

But that was her problem. Ax didn't look too kindly on her either.

Eventually the feeling of being watched ebbed, and Ax went back to his observation.

The soldiers didn't do anything interesting.

Unlike Aorsa, Kilrym had day and night, light and dark, at all times of the year. And eventually darkness fell and he and Luci headed back to catch some sleep.

But a sense of dread suffused Ax. Something was bound to go wrong. And he had no idea how he and Luci were going to get out of this thing alive.

19

Luci: I used to drive to clear my head. I miss it.
Ax: You can use my vehicle any time.

THANK God that Zulir cars functioned basically the same way as cars did back on Earth. Luci would have been absolutely no help to Ax if there was some special space car she needed to learn how to drive.

That was her job right now. Getaway driver. Or it would be in a few minutes. She and Ax were huddled in the woods and watching the Apsyns and waiting to see when they were ready to hand off the technology. As soon as it started, Luci would run for the vehicle they had found and appropriated for their mission. She was going to cut off access down the road and trap them.

At least that was the plan. She had no idea if things would actually end up going well.

They had an idea of which way the Apsyns were going, but they weren't sure. If they were right, she would be able to just pull the vehicle out of its hiding place and park so she blocked the two lane road that led to the city. If they were wrong... Well, she didn't want to think about what would happen if they were wrong.

Ax had been insistent. There were only two of them. They didn't get to plan for the perfect mission. All they got to do was make up something on the fly and hope it worked.

Luci really hoped it worked. Now that she was bonded to Ax, she couldn't imagine what it would feel like if some sort of technology ripped that apart. It might have been done hastily. It might have been something that she hadn't wanted a week ago. But she had it now, and she wanted it, and she wasn't letting it go.

The large bay doors of the warehouse opened, and a vehicle rolled out.

"Do you think they're driving it to the city?" Luci asked.

Ax gave a tight nod. "That's good. That means no one's coming to pick it up. No extra combatants."

Right. That was good. Luci tried to remind herself of that fact.

"Get ready to run," Ax warned her. As soon as the car started moving, she would have to run. It wasn't far. Another symptom of the bonding was that Luci and Ax couldn't be too far from one another if they wanted their powers to work. They could manage a couple of miles' distance, probably, but they weren't sure. And they didn't want to be surprised.

The vehicle pulled onto the road and pointed in the direction they expected. One of the Apsyns was already in the car and another one came out carrying the bag that Hanna had delivered to them.

"Go," Ax commanded.

Luci went. She wasn't much of a runner. If she sprinted too far, her lungs gave out, and she wanted to just collapse onto the side of the track and huddle into a ball and pretend that she would never have to run again. But that was gym class. This was real life. And if she didn't run today, millions of people would be hurt.

She ran like her life and her heart and her entire existence depended on it. And in a few minutes, she was at the car and pulling out of the brush that was hiding it to block off the road. They couldn't just leave the car like that. Not when they hadn't known whether or not Apsyns were coming from the city to pick up the package. But now it was their only barricade.

Luci climbed back out of the vehicle and darted

towards her cover in the woods. That had been the next instruction that Ax had given her.

The Apsyns were likely to attack the vehicle once they saw it blocking the road, and since she didn't have any sort of special driving skills, she needed to be out of the vehicle and safe.

Or as safe as she could be.

Ax would be coming right behind them. She just had to stay alive until he got there.

Luci hated waiting like this. She just wanted the battle to be over.

She wasn't far away. And she could hear the first yell as an attack began.

She could feel Ax pulling on their combined powers and using his spark. He was good at it. He would be able to fight them. Even if it was four on one.

Four on one. Those were terrible odds. She should never have let him do this alone.

What was she thinking?

But she had no other choice. He was the soldier. He had the skills. She was just a girl from Earth.

No, a woman. A woman from Earth who cared very deeply for the man who was protecting her down the road. If she were a little more headstrong, she might have marched back there and used her powers to give him cover.

But he wouldn't want that. They both knew the

stakes. If he could stop them there, that would be best. But even if they got away and got down the road, they would have another chance.

She heard tires squeal. The Apsyns were coming.

Did that mean Ax was—

No. He wasn't dead. She would feel it. They were connected on a molecular level. If something happened to him, she would know it. Maybe not exactly what it was. But she would feel it deep inside of her.

Luci sunk deeper into her hiding place. She felt completely exposed, even if she was fairly certain she couldn't be seen. She heard the roar of an engine cut off suddenly. They were there.

They were at the car. They didn't ram it. So that was probably for the best.

"What in Braznon's bowels is this?" She heard muffled voices come from the road.

"Looks like that punting nuisance has help," said another voice.

"The road is too narrow to go around. We will end up in the ditch. Get inside and drive that thing off the road," the first voice commanded.

She couldn't hear what his partner said in reply, but she heard a car door slam and figured he was doing what had been commanded of him.

So there were at least two people out there. Maybe more in the vehicle. There could have been a total of four, Luci knew. But were there? Had two stayed behind to fight Ax?

That was the problem with really good hiding spaces. She couldn't see to get an idea of who was out there.

Footsteps crunched over leaves, and Luci knew one of them was in the woods.

"Where are you?" the Apsyn demanded. "Show yourself and I will show mercy."

She almost snorted in disbelief, but that would give away her position. Apsyns didn't know mercy. She would not let herself fall into their hands.

"You can't hide. Not for long."

Luci would hide forever if she had to. She closed her eyes and breathed deep. She could summon her spark if she concentrated. She wouldn't have more than one shot. But with the Apsyn moving slowly and trying to find her, she could hit him. If she could see him.

Ax would kill her if he knew what she was thinking, but she put thoughts of him aside. She crawled carefully, her fingers sinking into the dirt all around her. And then she got a glimpse of dark boots. He was closer than she thought. She stopped breathing. If she moved anymore, if she made any noise, she might summon him right to her.

Not good. Not good. Not good.

Her spark was right there. All she needed to do

was send it out to him. He was standing just as still as the target. But he wouldn't be for long.

If she failed, he was going to catch her.

But Ax was going to come for her. She was sure of it.

Luci summoned her spark and sent it out in a bolt straight at the Apsyn soldier. It hit, and he went down with a grunt.

She must have been stronger than she thought. He was breathing, but he wasn't conscious. And she didn't know how long that would last. Another wave of bravery came over her and she grabbed his blaster from its holster and stuck it into the pocket of her jeans. Then she grabbed the communicator he had pinned to his shoulder. She wasn't going to use it, but she didn't want him using it either.

She didn't know if there was anything else she should grab, and she wasn't going to risk staying around longer.

She considered the weight of the blaster in her pocket. If she shot him a few times, he wouldn't be getting back up.

It was tempting. Oh so tempting. The Apsyns had tried to destroy her, and she could take out this bit of vengeance on them with a few clicks of a button.

But killing an unarmed and unconscious man was a line she could not cross. That would make her a monster. She wasn't going to do it.

She turned back toward the road. With the blaster a surer shot than her spark, she could provide some help if Ax would get his ass over here.

She heard movement at the edge of the woods, but it wasn't Ax.

"Stay right where you are," the Apsyn soldier demanded. "Hands in the air."

AX WAS DRENCHED in sweat and on the edge of burning through all of his power. Bonded Zulir had a lot of power to use, but fighting four soldiers was his limit.

It got a little bit easier when two of them got in the vehicle and sped off in the direction of the city. Luci's vehicle would cut them off. But he had to unentangle himself from this mess before long. He didn't want those soldiers finding Luci.

Ax sent a big blast of his spark straight at the warehouse. He knew it wouldn't do anything to hurt the soldiers directly, but one of the walls collapsed, and that was enough to split their attention.

He took off running and dove into the woods. It would be faster to take the road, but he would be an easy target. He headed straight towards the car. The Apsyns had a few minutes on him and they had to already be there. But if Luci had stayed hidden like she was supposed to, then everything would be alright.

He burst out of the woods and saw two vehicles stopped in the center of the road with no Apsyns around them.

They were looking for Luci. That he was sure of.

He crossed the road to the other side, where Luci was supposed to be hiding, and saw the back of an Apsyn soldier with his wings flared and yelling at someone in the woods.

Ax didn't think. He struck out with his spark and flattened the man.

And then his mind went kind of fuzzy and his wings collapsed into his body. That was the last of his power. He was spent.

But the Apsyn went down. And as he fell, he revealed Luci standing right there with her hands in the air.

Her shoulders sagged as she saw Ax.

"Hey," she said.

A smile tugged at his lips. "Hey." What else was there to say? They were alive. They just had to figure out a way off of this planet.

Footsteps pounded against pavement, and he realized the two other Apsyns had come this way.

Ax dug deep and tried to summon some of the spark, but there was no power there for him to use.

"What's wrong?" Luci asked, putting a hand on his shoulder and giving him a squeeze.

He wanted to sag against her. He was flagging fast, and he didn't know how he was going to fight these two other soldiers. But he had to. Luci's life depended on it. "I used up my power."

"What does that mean?" Luci asked.

"Can't use my spark until I recharge." His whole body felt shaky, but he forced himself to remain standing. He wasn't going to fall and fail Luci.

He expected more questions, but she didn't ask any. Instead she reached into her pocket and handed him a small blaster, Apsyn issue. "I took it off one of those soldiers. I used my spark to flatten him. Will this help?"

He kissed her. He couldn't resist. But it had to be fast. The soldiers would find them at any minute. And the two in the woods were still alive. At least he thought they were. He didn't know how long they'd be unconscious.

"Stay behind me," he commanded.

Luci took a deep breath and her wings flared out behind her. They were beautiful, a collection of purples and blues and bright whites. He wanted to stare at them all day. But he couldn't get distracted.

"Keep close to me," Luci said. "I'll cover you."

It went against every instinct he had. He wanted to keep her safe. But her wings could act as a shield, and with his power running so dangerously low, he really needed it right now. So he didn't argue.

They had to get the package from the Apsyn vehicle and then get into their own vehicle and drive off somewhere safe without being caught. It should have been easy. Ax knew it would be anything but. Especially with two soldiers out on the road waiting for them.

"We have to take them out," he warned Luci. "It's going to be fast. Are you ready?"

She gave a grim nod. "Do what you have to do."

Ax raised his blaster.

He stepped out of the woods just in time to see the two soldiers fall, hit by an almost impossibly bright flash of spark.

Hanna stepped out from behind one of the vehicles.

"Do you guys want to get out of here?"

20

Luci: I think I made a friend today.

Ax: Good for you. Anyone would be lucky to know you.

Luci, Ax, and Hanna stared at each other in silence for several seconds. What was she doing here? Why had she attacked those Apsyns?

Why had she worked with them in the first place?

The questions all got caught in the back of Luci's throat, and she didn't say anything. She reached deep inside of herself and summoned as much of her spark as she could. Ax was tapped out. He looked ready to fall over at any moment, even if he gripped his blaster tight in his hand. Hanna was a hell of a fighter. And she wasn't exhausted. But Luci wasn't going to let her take her man.

"Are you just going to stand there?" Hanna demanded.

"I don't know, are you going to kidnap us again?" Luci couldn't have stopped the jab if she wanted to.

"That was a coincidence. We're on the same side. And I let you off the space ship, didn't I? I didn't give you over to them when I had the chance." She said it like she was making some grand point.

Luci's eyes widened, and her mouth dropped open in indignation. "You *let* us escape? Are you crazy? And I've never willingly worked with the Apsyns. I would say we're on completely different sides." She couldn't believe that she had hoped to have a friendship with this woman. Anyone who would work with the Apsyns was a monster. Or at least they condoned monstrous things.

Hanna's expression shifted to a scowl. "Grow up, little girl. I didn't have to let you escape my ship. I didn't have to save you just now. You *owe* me."

"You're out of line," Ax said, taking half a step in front of Luci to shield her from Hanna.

Luci appreciated it, but she was the one with wings, and she wrapped them around Ax to keep Hanna from doing anything violent.

The Apsyn woman tipped her head back and laughed. "This is rich. A human/Zulir pairing. They would kill you on sight if they saw you."

"We're not the only human/Synnr Match." Luci

didn't know why she felt so defensive. The Apsyns hated humans. Of course they would hate the pairing. Of course Hanna was no different.

Hanna stared at her for a moment and shrugged. She didn't acknowledge the other pairings, which she must have known about if she'd lived on Aorsa for some time. It was no secret there. The Apsyns knew full well that humans and Zulir were compatible. "I can get you off the planet," Hanna said.

In the distance, Luci heard an engine rumble and hoped it wasn't someone coming their way. Did the soldiers have backup? Was someone expecting them this soon?

Her first instinct was to reject the deal out of hand. She didn't trust Hanna. Hanna would have killed her if it had come down to that. It didn't matter that she had just saved their lives. She couldn't be trusted.

But Ax put a hand on her wrist to quiet her. "In exchange for what?" he asked.

Hanna gave him a flat stare. "Nothing your precious morals can't handle. Simply speak for me to the authorities. Tell them what you know."

"So you want me to tell them that you kidnapped us and transported us to Apsyn territory in the middle of a war?" Ax asked, voice dripping with sarcasm.

Hanna narrowed her eyes. "I didn't know *you*

were on my ship. And I was never planning to turn her over to the Apsyns. That was… an unfortunate necessity. I always planned to send little Luci back to Aorsa. But you saw that I fought those Apsyns, but I helped you recover the technology."

Luci bristled at Hanna's tone. Had she been holding back vitriol all this time? "Technology that you stole in the first place," she couldn't help but add.

Hanna shrugged. "I am not your enemy. I have intelligence that could be helpful to the Synnrs. And I am no friend of the Apsyns."

"You're a spy," Ax accused.

"I was a freelancer," she countered. "Hired for one job. They weren't too forthcoming about what the job was, and as soon as I found out, you saw my reaction."

Luci and Ax backed up a few steps until they were far enough away that Hanna couldn't hear them. They didn't have much time to make a choice. They didn't know if the Apsyn soldiers had friends coming, and the sooner they could get away the better.

And, if they didn't play nice with Hanna, she could probably call down more Apsyn soldiers on them. Luci wasn't sure she believed the whole freelancer gig.

"You can't be thinking of trusting her," she told Ax. There were bags under his eyes and he looked ready to drop. She wanted to find a place where he could rest. He had done the heavy lifting for the past several days. She wanted to get them home and get them into his bed and then tend to him like the good girlfriend she planned to be. Did Synnrs like chicken noodle soup? She was going to find out.

"What are other options?" Ax asked. He didn't sound tired, no matter how bad he looked. She knew he was putting on a brave face for her.

On instinct more than anything else, Luci pushed some of her own spark through the connection that bound them together and sent it to Ax. Awareness zinged through him, and he stood up a little straighter, shooting her a grin.

"Be careful," he warned. "Give me too much and you will be the one passed out."

"I've got power to spare," she promised. "Didn't you say you had friends on the planet? Who could get us away from here?"

He grimaced. "I can't guarantee it. She seems pretty certain she can get us off planet. She's not even asking us to lie."

"But how can we trust her?" Did he not remember all of the crap that Hanna had done? She would rather hide out in a cave on Kilrym for months until they could get a proper extraction than trust Hanna anymore.

But Ax still looked tired, and he was the one with

connections on this planet. "She might be our only shot," said Ax.

Luci didn't want to hear that. She wanted some miracle to show up, a magically abandoned speeder that could get them between Kilrym and Aorsa without anyone being the wiser.

But they had used up a lot of miracles on their survival to this point. And maybe Hanna was a blessing in disguise. Luci hated to think it, but what else could she be?

"I don't like it," she had to say.

"You think I do?" Ax asked.

"Are you sure about this?" Luci really wanted to say no. Hanna was bad news.

"No. But we don't have another choice."

He was right, dammit. Why was he right? Luci hated it. She looked over her shoulder back at Hanna, who was waiting patiently. No, not so patiently. While Luci and Ax had been talking, Hanna had grabbed the duffel bag from inside the Apsyns' vehicle and it now sat at her feet.

"That little…"

"What?" Ax asked, following her gaze. Then he saw it. "You're not taking that," he informed Hanna.

She crossed her arms. "And you're going to stop me?" She looked at him for several seconds and then down at the bag. Then she sent a blinding flash of her spark at the bag, destroying the whole thing, bag and contents. "It's all yours."

For a moment, Luci felt another searing jolt of betrayal before she realized what Hanna had done. No one could have the technology now. Maybe there was a backup of it somewhere. Maybe it could be rebuilt. But whatever she had stolen from the University of Aorsa was gone. No Matches were going to be destroyed.

And that was for the best. Not even the Apsyns deserved that fate.

"If you try and betray us, we will kill you," Luci warned.

For some reason that made Hanna laugh. "I wouldn't expect anything less. Now come on."

HANNA DROVE. Ax didn't like it, but she was the one who knew where they were going. Apparently she had a ride off the planet, and they didn't have long to get wherever they were going.

Ax didn't have much energy left to complain. The small jolt of Luci's spark was the pick me up he'd needed to keep one foot in front of the other for a little while. But soon enough, he knew he was going to collapse in an unconscious heap until his spark regenerated. That was the risk of using too much power. But he had to make sure Luci was safe first.

He kept looking out the back window, waiting to see if Apsyns would follow them. There was no one on the dusty old road that they traveled on.

The smell of fried electric parts permeated the inside of the vehicle. He could barely admit it, but he was glad Hanna had destroyed the device. Ax would have been honor bound to turn it over to the Synnr military. But it was something so destructive that he hoped no one ever figured out how to use it. A Match was a blessing, even for the Apsyns. And they didn't deserve to be destroyed like that.

He questioned Hanna's motives.

What did she want? Who was she really working for? But it wasn't for him to figure out. Once they got to Aorsa, she would be arrested. He and Luci could be as well. They'd been gone for days, and someone might have assumed they had deserted.

Or at least that he had. He would do anything to make sure Luci didn't face consequences for this.

It was another few minutes before they pulled into an airfield which had four rockets sitting and waiting for takeoff.

"There's a hooded jacket back there," Hanna said, gesturing at them. "Luci, put it on. We don't want anyone seeing what you really are."

Ax bristled at her tone, and Luci's eyes got fired

up with anger, but a moment later she dug out the sweater and put it on, pulling the hood up until her face was shrouded in shadow. Humans and Zulir looked enough alike that from a distance no one could tell the difference. But if someone at this airfield found out that two Zulir were trying to take a human off the planet, there might be questions. Questions that neither he nor Hanna would want to answer.

Technically, there was a lot of paperwork that should be filled out, but Ax had a feeling that Hanna knew which palms to grease to make sure that paperwork was the least of their worries.

Hanna parked the vehicle and the three of them got out, their only luggage the fried duffel bag filled with destroyed metal parts.

An old Zulir mechanic greeted Hanna and only gave Ax and Luci quick looks before looking away. The kind of look a person shot another person when they didn't want to remember who they were seeing. This was the kind of airfield that did plenty of business with criminals, Ax was sure. Maybe smugglers, pirates, slavers. People who didn't want questions asked.

Hanna was proving more and more interesting. The old Zulir man pointed them towards one of the rockets, and the three of them were off. But they only made it a few paces when the man called after them.

"Authorities are looking hard at humans escaping the planet. It would be a shame for you to get shot down over something so trifling."

Was that a warning or threat? Ax took a step closer to Luci. He still had that blaster, and he could shoot the man before he had a chance to act against them.

"Noted," said Hanna.

"You can catch a fair price for a human," the man added.

"Noted," Hanna said again, voice cold.

Would she try and sell Luci to this man? Ax waited. It went against all his instincts, but they were so close. He didn't want to shoot first and make a giant mistake.

Eventually the man shrugged and walked off. Hanna led them to the rocket.

Luci didn't say anything, but Ax saw that her hands were shaking. He put an arm around her and held her close.

The ship they were in was designed for short haul trips between Kilrym and its moon. It wasn't anything fancy, but it would get them home.

Hanna took her place in the cockpit. "You two can go find a room. Get some sleep. This will all be over soon."

"Yeah, right," Luci said as she sank down into the copilot's seat.

Ax smiled at his Match's attitude and took a seat in the navigator's chair. He wasn't letting Hanna out of his sight either.

But she didn't argue. She engaged the thrusters, and a few minutes later, they were off.

The military checked in with them for a proper exit code, and Hanna gave them a number that Ax didn't recognize. This was another chance for a betrayal. And now there was no place that he or Luci could run.

But the military cleared them through. And soon they were home free.

Aorsa was in their sights. But what fate awaited them when they were finally home?

Ax: There's no sweeter sight than Aorsa on a viewscreen as you come into orbit.

THE FLIGHT TOOK HOURS, and Ax kept waiting for Hanna to betray them. But she flew the speeder with confidence and never gave a hint that anything was wrong. He started to feel relief as Aorsa became visible and large in the view screen. Home. This nightmare was almost over.

"Send out a message," he told Hanna. "We don't want to get shot down right now."

She opened a line of communication and Ax took over, giving his full name and identification in the hopes that it would smooth their path.

It did.

They were directed to a field and given a time to

land. And once they broke atmo, two Synnr vehicles accompanied them all the way to the ground. The Synnrs were not going to risk this ship getting away.

Ax had a bad feeling about it. Here he was showing up in an Apsyn vehicle after days away. They had to know that something was wrong. But would they trust him?

He hoped so. He needed that to be true.

Hanna set the ship down and then looked over at Ax. "We had a deal," she reminded him.

"I know." He would do exactly what he needed to do. Luci had fallen asleep, and he gently shook her to wake her up. She looked so cute right then that he felt guilty, but they were home, and he would let her sleep in his bed for as long as she wanted. But they had to get off the ship.

"We're there?" she asked, blinking the sleep out of her eyes.

"Yes," Ax answered.

That seemed to wake Luci up. She got out of her chair and rolled her head from side to side, stretching out sore muscles. "Thank God. Let's get out of here."

Ax smiled. Hanna seemed to be steeling herself for what was to come, and Ax felt a momentary pang of sympathy for her. Yes, she had brought all of this on herself, but she was walking straight into the consequences. It had to be hard. But he wasn't going to let her get away.

Hanna took a deep breath before she opened the hatch, and she had both of her hands raised in surrender as she walked down the steps and onto the ground.

Aorsa.

Synnr ground.

Home.

Half a dozen soldiers, Jori included, had their blasters raised and pointed at the three of them. Ax put his own hands up, and a quick glance at Luci had her raising her hands as well.

"What's going on, Ax?" Jori demanded. He had his wings out and his blaster pointed. He meant business.

"It wasn't a vacation," Ax shot back. Of course, now was not the time to be making jokes, but it was Jori. They were friends.

"Ax." Jori wasn't impressed.

"Well, it all starts with Hanna here." Ax gave the rundown as well as he could. And there was a small part of him that was tempted to leave out some of the details from what happened on Kilrym. He already didn't go into detail about what he and Luci had done between themselves. Sure, he explained the bonding and the survival. But the soldiers didn't need to know anything else about their relationship. But at the end, he also added that Hanna had saved their lives and provided them transportation. It wasn't a great report. She was still likely to be thrown in prison for her actions. But if he had to guess, she wouldn't be executed.

Jori stared at the three of them for several moments before finally holstering his blaster. He didn't pull in his wings. "Take the woman into custody. Not Luci."

Two Synnrs came forward and grabbed Hanna, slapping her into manacles and leading her toward a waiting vehicle. The other soldiers holstered their weapons, and three of the four of them pulled in their wings. Though Ax hadn't managed to sleep, some of his energy was replenished. But he wasn't going to be fighting his own people.

"Welcome home," said Jori. "Major Ozar wants to see you. Both of you."

Punt. He looked over at Luci. "We can't go home yet."

LUCI WANTED TO GO HOME. And this time, her first thought of home wasn't Earth. It was Ax's bed. She'd lost track of time hours ago. Or maybe minutes. That was the problem with losing track of time. There was no real way to actually know how much time had passed.

But it had been *forever*. Jori had taken her and Ax back to headquarters and separated them.

Luci didn't like that. After so many days with only Ax keeping her standing, it was strange to be separated.

She would have to get used to that. At least a little. And she could comfort herself with the feeling of the bond that burned bright between them.

But she wanted him back.

The Synnrs didn't seem to care. They stuck her in a room and made her wait while Ax was off doing God knew what. She didn't know if anyone was going to tell her anything. But eventually the door opened and she was excited, certain she was about to be allowed to go home.

But it was no such thing. Emily Saint and Malsan Ozar walked in the room and took a seat. Emily was one of the humans who had been rescued from Kilrym with her. She was bonded to Oz, a Synnr warrior. And if they were both coming to talk to her, Luci knew this whole thing was far from over.

"What's going on? Is something wrong?" She wanted to break out of the room and find Ax, but that was just going to get her thrown into a cell or something like that.

"Nothing's wrong," Emily assured her. She glanced back at Oz, who gave her a nod. "But Ax told us about your Match and your bonding. And we needed to talk to you about that."

"About what?" It was none of their business. Ax was hers, and she wasn't giving him back. No one could break the bond. They had destroyed the only tech that would allow that to happen, and good riddance.

"Down girl," Emily said. "No one's taking him away from you. But there are certain… expectations that go along with a bond to a Synnr warrior. And we wanted to answer any questions before you're given your first assignment."

"Assignment?" Emily wasn't talking about school.

"You'll be in training at first. They know you're not a warrior. But part of the bonding means that Ax has a limited range of powers. At least when it comes to you. You need to be in close proximity to one another for them to work."

"I know that." She knew what she had known about Matching, and she was sure she would learn more as things went on.

"I want to help you," said Emily. "I know what it's like to be a human suddenly thrust into this world. I was hoping to… Never mind. I just want to help."

Emily had taken Luci under her wing, her metaphorical wing at the time, when they were held prisoner. Emily had been like the big sister Luci never had. But she'd also treated Luci like a kid for a very long time. She wasn't looking at her like a kid now. She was looking at her like a woman whose life was about to change dramatically. And Luci was really wishing she could go back to being that kid again. But childhood was over. It was time to grow up.

"Can I stay in school?" University was important to her. It was her way of making a life for herself in this place so far from where she'd been born. She didn't regret bonding with Ax, but she didn't want to give up everything.

"I'm sure we can find a way to work something out," said Oz. "You may need to take a later schedule, and you might have some absences. But we'll get you that education."

Luci didn't know if she felt relieved or disappointed. All of her emotions were crashing down on her, and she couldn't quite get a hold on them. She wanted to laugh or cry, and she definitely wanted to sleep. It was only now dawning on her that she had survived an ordeal. It was the kind of thing that most people never dreamed of.

And that had just been her life for the past six months. One ordeal after another. She could sleep for a year and it wouldn't be enough.

"I'll do what I have to do," she told Emily and Oz. "I just want to go home right now."

Emily took pity on her and gave her a soft smile.

"We just have a few more things to go over with you. Then we'll let you go."

Emily was true to her word. They went over the basics of what it meant to be a newly bonded Match, a human with Zulir powers. Luci had a worksheet she was supposed to fill out and some basic instructions on how to use her powers. It would give her a starting off point before she officially entered warrior training in the next week or two. She wouldn't be directly in combat if she didn't want to be, but they would have to test her range when it came to Ax to see what he could do as well.

And then finally Emily and Oz let her go. When Luci saw a clock on the wall, she realized it had been hours since she and Ax had gotten off the ship. She looked around the building, which at this hour was mostly deserted, and she didn't see Ax.

Had he gone home without her? She wandered the halls, looking for him. She didn't think he would have left without her. She hoped he wouldn't have. But she remembered some of the things that she had said to him before they had left Aorsa and ended up on Kilrym. They hadn't been nice. They hadn't been the kind of things that someone who loved another person said to them.

She hoped he didn't think that things would just go back to the way they'd been before Kilrym. She was a different person now. Stronger. And she wanted Ax with all her heart.

She turned the corner and there he was, coming out of the room, the bags under his eyes huge, but the smile on his face was enough to make up for it.

She didn't know she could feel that much relief from such a small thing as seeing her boyfriend.

Her mate?

She would have to figure out the terminology later.

"Want to get out of here?" Ax asked.

"Let's go home."

2 2

Luci: When I text you, you're supposed to text back. That's etiquette.
Ax: Noted.

LUCI HAD HER COMMUNICATOR BACK, which was a relief. In the chaos of getting on Hanna's ship and their adventure to Kilrym and back, she had sort of forgotten about it. It had run out of battery shortly after Ax found it, and she didn't remember him mentioning it when they were on the planet.

That probably was something they should have talked about, but their minds had been otherwise occupied and she couldn't blame him.

But now the communicator had a full charge, and Luci had access to all of her contacts. Her friends were probably worried about her. They probably wanted her back home and safe where they could see her. But that wasn't where she was going.

Luci opened up her messages, and before she could send one out, she saw all the words that had flown back and forth between her and Ax before their abduction. The thread went on and on, hundreds of little messages, sweet and sultry enough to make her blush. But they weren't just sexual in nature. They shared their thoughts and jokes and hopes and dreams.

It was proof that the thing between them had always been more than casual. Luci was just too scared to see it before. But she saw it now and she wasn't afraid. She and Ax were powerful together and perfect. She wouldn't give that up for the world.

As she and Ax drove through the streets of Aorsa, she pulled up a contact and made a call.

Gayle answered quickly. "Luci? What's going on? Where are you?" The questions were fast like punches, and Luci felt the blow.

"I'm okay. I'm okay," she assured the older woman. "I'm not sure what I'm allowed to tell you. But I am on Aorsa. I'm safe. And everything's fine."

"On *Aorsa*? Were you not here?" She sounded flummoxed. "I just assumed you were locked away with your boyfriend for a week. Was this not a sexcapade?"

A laugh burst out of Luci at the question. "I wish.

Ax and I ran into a bit of trouble. And it turns out we're a Match. We're bonded now. And we're headed back to his place for the night."

Gayle was quiet for so long that Luci wondered if the call had dropped.

"Hello?"

"You're not telling me a lot." It wasn't a question.

Luci's cheeks heated. She wanted to tell Gayle the whole story. But she knew once she told one of the humans, all of them would know. And Emily and Oz had impressed on her the need for discretion during their discussion about what it meant to work for the Synnr military.

"Isn't it just important that I'm safe?" Luci asked.

"I'm glad you're safe. I assume you would be telling me more if you could. But I expect a good story when you come back. So you and Ax, huh?"

Luci didn't even feel the urge to groan in embarrassment this time. She knew her feelings. She knew what she wanted. And she was heading to exactly where she wanted to be. "Yeah. Me and Ax."

"So the next time you come to the house, are you just getting your stuff to go move in with your honey bunny? Pretty soon this place is going to feel empty." Gayle didn't sound too disappointed at having more room to herself.

That shocked silence out of Luci. Moving in with Ax? She hadn't really thought about that. And she wasn't sure how to answer. "Uhhhh... we'll talk about that later."

Gayle laughed loud enough that Luci had to pull the communicator away from her ear with a wince. That was enough. Gayle promised to let everyone know that Luci was out of harm's way, and then she threatened that everyone would have questions the next time Luci showed up. But that was the price she had to pay for having friends. Luci disengaged the call and stuck her communicator in her pocket.

"Everything alright?" Ax asked, reaching over and threading their fingers together.

It could be like this, she realized. Her and Ax together, peacefully. She had never imagined anything so wonderful.

"I think they're going to tease me the next time they see me. I might have been a bit adamant about what I thought I wanted."

"Oh yeah?" Ax deserved an award for how even he managed to keep his tone.

She was never going to live this down. "Shut up."

"I didn't say anything."

"Say anything more and we're breaking up."

He laughed.

Some threat that was. She had fallen for him so hard that she couldn't imagine even pretending to break up. He was everything she wanted. Why would she let that go when she was finally happy?

Yeah, it came with a cost. But so did everything. And yeah it meant that her life wasn't going to be what she had imagined. But the plan had changed a long time ago, and Luci was learning that the plan didn't always matter. It was what she made of the road she traveled down.

By the time they made it to Ax's place, Luci's eyes were heavy and she was stumbling up the stairs to his door. They stripped off their clothes and made it to the bedroom, where they fell on the bed. Luci pulled Ax close and started to kiss him.

They were finally home safe. She wanted to savor this time with him for as long as they had it. She didn't know when she would get called in for training or when they would be sent off on a mission. She didn't know how much time they would have alone together for the foreseeable future.

But her body was already heavy with exhaustion, and no matter how hard she kissed him, she couldn't take it any further.

Ax held her close and they both drifted off to sleep. And somehow that was even better than the alternative.

***

LUCI WANTED to wake up in Ax's arms.

Her mate, it appeared, had other ideas. She

slowly came to consciousness, all comfy and warm in his bed, but as she stretched, she realized she was alone. She frowned. Not exactly the romantic awakening she'd imagined after their adventure.

She took a minute to revel in safety. There were no Apsyn soldiers trying to hunt them. No one was going to kidnap her. She and Ax had nothing to fear. At least for the next few hours. There were new problems to consider with her duties as Ax's Match, but she would worry about those later.

Right now she needed to find her man.

Luci pushed the covers off and followed the sound of running water to the bathroom, where heat and steam permeated everything. And there Ax was, standing under the spray with water running down his naked body.

Yum.

She took a minute to look at him, eyes skimming over those muscles and the water making his iridescent skin practically shine. She'd wanted him from the first moment she had woken up enough from the horror of what had been done to her to actually want anything. And now he was all hers.

His hands soaped up his body in efficient strokes, but her fingers itched to touch him. She must have made a noise. Ax turned and smiled at her, hands stilling as he watched her through the mist of the shower.

"Good morning," he said.

"It could be better." Luci grinned as she tugged off her clothes and approached the shower, sliding the door open and joining her man. She yelped at the heat, but her body quickly adjusted. "It's like standing under a lava flow."

Ax chuckled and turned the heat down just a bit. "Better?"

"I think you'll need to kiss it for it to be better." He was confused for a second, and Luci realized that the Earth phrase might not make sense to his ears, but the confusion cleared as carnal intent lit his eyes.

She shivered despite the heat. She loved that look in Ax's eyes.

He leaned down and kissed her, pulling her close and clutching their bodies together. Luci relaxed against him, finally feeling right. She wanted to be with him, wanted to wake up beside him and carve out a life together.

Her spark fizzed through her veins at the thought, but she kept it caged. Probably not best to mix electricity and water. Or maybe it was okay. Ax's tongue swiped against hers, and the thought disappeared.

Much better to kiss her man.

Yes.

That.

The heat of the shower only served to loosen her

body as a different kind of heat suffused her. She wrapped her legs around Ax, glad for the friction mat on the floor which kept him from slipping. He pushed her back against the wall, and Luci moaned against him as his cock brushed her sensitive flesh.

He fit himself to her entrance and slowly slid in, water pouring down his back like they were caught in a sensual rainstorm.

Luci loved it.

And as Ax moved inside of her, she gave herself fully over to the pleasure, letting it roll over her in waves as her body found new ways to feel everything he was giving to her.

Her spark reached out for his through their bond, the power still caged inside of them, but mingling invisibly. She couldn't see it, but she undeniably felt it. She sent a surge toward Ax, and he groaned in pleasure and sent a jolt in response that made her gasp.

Oh, they were going to have fun with that.

It was a mix of their sparks and their merged bodies that sent Luci over the edge, clutching Ax's shoulders and crying out as she came. He followed soon behind.

They stayed in an embrace for some time after that. Luci's legs were shaky and her heart didn't want to let go of Ax just yet.

"That was almost better than coffee," she said, lips brushing his shoulder.

A laugh burst out of him. "Almost?"

Okay, so it was ten times better than coffee, but Luci wasn't about to admit that. "Really close," she responded.

They washed off, and when they got out of the shower, Ax tugged her back towards his bedroom rather than letting her gather her clothes. "I'll show you almost better than coffee." He scooped her up and set her on the bed, sending her bouncing on the mattress.

Luci yelped and laughed and then sighed happily into the kiss as Ax came down on top of her, water dripping from his hair. Their second joining was slower, less frantic than the shower, but somehow even more intimate.

Luci wanted to say things to him, but every word got swallowed up in a kiss, and eventually she realized that was even better than words. She could show him what she felt with her body.

And show him she did. And if his body was anything to go by, he felt exactly the same.

There were places to be and duties to attend to, but all of that faded to nothingness as she and Ax were joined. She was finally happy and the world could wait.

23

Luci: I'm ready to be happy.

THE CAMPUS LOOKED EXACTLY the same as Luci remembered it. Of course it did. She'd been gone less than a week. But she noticed more students smiling at her and greeting her. Her classes didn't seem as difficult. And she was optimistic about how the year would go.

Was it a new attitude? Were people sensing the change in her?

She wasn't going to look too closely at it. There was no need to over analyze every aspect of her life. She was done doing that. She was just going to enjoy things while they lasted.

Luckily she'd only needed to make up one assignment for her math class. It was a little disappointing that Hanna was no longer there. But Hanna had always just been a figment of Luci's imagination. A cipher who pretended to be her friend.

And she had been replaced by someone much more enjoyable.

Zac sat in the middle of the classroom and moved his bag off a seat when he saw Luci.

"I can't believe you convinced me to take a math class," he said. The human man had been an English literature PhD candidate back on Earth. Apparently he and math were old nemeses.

"It's fun... sort of." Okay, that was an exaggeration. It was still math, and Luci still had her issues with it. But she was just happy to be able to take the class.

"Did you get your schedule worked out?" Zac asked.

"I had to drop three classes, and it's going to take quite a while to get this degree. But they're willing to work with my schedule." It had taken some wrangling and a lot of calendar studying, but Luci was pretty sure her new schedule would work.

"Great."

She and Zac were both taking a hybrid approach to their attendance at the University of Aorsa. Since they were both bonded to warriors, her to Ax and Zac to both Crowze and Grace, they had duties with the Synnr military that couldn't be ignored or even really scheduled. But that didn't mean they had to completely dedicate their lives to military service. Neither of them were warriors and they had to forge their own paths.

It was good to have Zac on campus with her. He seemed to have the ability to make friends with just about anyone, or at least to engage them in conversation. Luci shouldn't have been surprised. The man had befriended the Synnr Queen. And that took some skill.

And because of him, she had started to make connections with her fellow students, and she and Zac had a standing lunch date with two other Synnrs who went to the university.

It was great. And it was real.

The professor showed up and a hush fell over the class, their conversations quieting as it was time to get down to work.

After class, she and Zac headed off campus, taking the vehicle that Zac was driving. They headed toward the training facility where they were both learning how to master their sparks and be useful to their Matches.

"Do you regret it?" Zac asked.

What a strange question to ask.

She'd woken up in Ax's arms and left his place after a searing kiss that had her considering skipping class. She'd never been happier in her entire life. "Not a bit. You?"

Zac grinned and blushed. "I wouldn't trade it for anything." They went their separate ways and Luci headed toward the locker room to change into her training clothes. She was about to sweat. Hard. And she didn't want to get her nice school clothes dirty.

She concentrated for a second and let her wings flare out. It was still amazing to consider that she had a spark of her own, powers of her own. But they were right there and they were all hers. She couldn't wait to figure out how to properly harness her power, and once she was changed, she headed down the hallway to meet with her training instructor.

It was time to get to work.

Ax FOUND Jori as he was heading out of one of the interrogation rooms, a dark look on his face. Jori had been one of the Synnrs tasked with getting information out of Hanna. It had been several days, and every time Ax saw him, Jori's mood was darker and darker.

"How's it going?" Ax asked. He didn't expect Jori to give him details, but they were friends, and clearly Jori needed to vent.

But Jori just scowled and said, "I don't want to

talk about it."

His tone was enough to stop Ax in his tracks. "That bad?"

"I don't want to talk about it," Jori repeated through clenched teeth.

That was clear enough. They wouldn't talk about it. If Jori changed his mind, he knew where to find Ax.

"How's Matched life treating you?" Jori asked, changing the subject with the subtlety of a wrecking ball.

Ax felt the smile bloom on his face. He didn't care how Jori changed the subject, not if it gave him a chance to think about his mate. "Things are going well. You should consider putting your data in for a Match. It's nothing like I ever imagined."

Jori groaned. "Don't start with that. I swear. The second anyone gets Matched, that's all they can talk about. Did it never occur to you that some of us don't want a Match?"

Ax kept his mouth shut. Truly, no, it had never occurred to him that someone wouldn't want to Match ever. Why not? He wanted to know Jori's reasoning, but he didn't ask. The man was in a sour mood, and Ax had a feeling he was spoiling for a fight. And Ax was not going to be the person to give it to him.

"If you need any help with anything, you know

I'm here," he offered. Whether Jori needed help with Hanna or questions about Matching or anything in particular.

"Thanks for the offer. I need to go talk to Major Ozar. I'll see you later." The other man left before Ax could do much more than wave.

He checked his watch and saw it was just about time for Luci's training to be finished. He headed off toward the changing rooms and waited outside the one he knew that Luci preferred. A few minutes later, she came out, her hair damp and her skin with the kind of glow that only came from strenuous exercise.

"You're a sight for sore eyes," she told him, using one of those funny Earth phrases. "If you were my trainer, I swear I might have cried."

Ax smiled and pulled her close, kissing her forehead. "I do have a few exercises in mind for you." He let the seduction thread his words.

Luci made a noise that went straight to his cock, and Ax regretted saying anything while they were still in the training facility. "Let's head back home."

"We promised to have dinner with everyone at Human House." Luci winced as she said it.

Ax regretted that he couldn't take his mate right back home to have his way with her, but a sense of satisfaction suffused him at what she said. She hadn't officially moved into his apartment in the weeks since they'd been back on Aorsa. But more and more of her things seemed to be appearing in his closet. And she didn't object when he called it home.

He wasn't going to push the subject. If she wanted to say something official, he was happy to oblige. Anything that kept her close.

"It will be good to share a meal with our friends."

"Can't we put it off?" she begged.

He wanted to. More than he could ever imagine. It didn't even bother him that everyone would know what they were doing instead. But he soldiered on. They had made plans and they would stick to them. "We'll make the most of our after dinner activities," he promised. "But they're our friends. We need to go."

"You're too considerate," she scowled.

"It's what you love about me," he teased.

"That and many other things," she admitted. "And don't pretend you don't love that I would totally ditch our friends so we could go fuck the night away."

"That and many things," he agreed, and he really considered ditching. But this dinner *was* important. And he and Luci would have plenty of time alone together later.

They clasped their hands and walked out of the building and to his waiting vehicle.

Ax just hoped dinner went fast. He had plans for his mate and he didn't want to wait.

24

JORI STOOD in front of the view screen that looked into Hanna's cell. It was a nice cell, as far as the facilities went. She had a cot and blankets. There was a sink and a small partition to give her privacy when she used the facilities.

A food processor was embedded in the wall and programmed to give her any meal she requested. She even had a tablet filled with entertainment, though it wasn't connected to any network.

It was more than she deserved.

Jori couldn't stand spies. They were the scum of the military, the lowest of the low. Though Hanna maintained she was no spy. She was merely a… what did she call it?

Freelancer.

He knew a lie when he heard it.

But still, she wasn't what he'd expected. And the information she was offering was more than helpful. He wouldn't be surprised if she was given some sort of deal that allowed her out of the cell before long. But he wouldn't trust her. She was up to something.

He was certain of it.

It was his job to get to the bottom of things. And he was going to find out what he needed to get her thrown into a cell for the rest of her days. He didn't want her free on the streets of Aorsa. He wasn't going to let her hurt anyone else.

She wasn't evil. She didn't seem too conniving. She seemed genuine.

And he was sure that was all a lie.

He was determined to figure out what she was hiding. And he would tear her mind apart if he had to do it.

Jori straightened his shoulders and rolled some of the tension out of his neck before pressing the button to open the door to her cell and begin another interrogation session.

She was not going to win this game.

Thank you for reading Synnr's Kiss!
I'd appreciate it so much if you would consider
leaving a review.

Can a man without emotions find his mate?

There's nothing left in Raze. No love, no hate, nothing but the duty that he owes his people. But when he meets a fascinating and tough human woman on a barren planet something deep inside comes back to life and for the first time in years he yearns for more.

Can she trust the ice cold warrior?

When a mission for the Sol Intelligence Agency gets out of hand, Sierra will need to use every skill she has and work with a mysterious alien warrior who awakens an unquenchable desire within her. He's cold and forbidding, but when he looks at her there's a fire in his eyes that opens up a whole world of possibilities.

Two worlds collide...

The chemistry between Raze and Sierra is too hot to ignore, even if it should be impossible for a mate bond to form between them. They'll need to fight pirates, their people, and fate itself to be together. But it may already be too late for the soulless warrior and the woman he aches to claim.

Download the ebook for free!

Also available in audio and paperback

Looking for something else? Kate Rudolph has a heart pounding collection or paranormal and sci-fi romance stories for you! Bundles, bears, audiobooks, aliens, and more. Check out your options in the list below. You can find out all you need to know at www.katerudolph.net.

Want to check out one of the books? Click on the series name to find out more!

Zulir Warrior Mates

Kidnapped humans. Alien Warriors. Electric wings.

The Zulir Warrior Mates series brings you human heroines and heroes abducted from Earth who find love – and wings! – with the alien warriors who rescue them.

Also available in audio!

Synnr's Saint

Synnr's Hope

Synnr's Spark

Synnr's Kiss

Guarded by the Shifter

Werewolf. Bodyguard. Mate.

The origins of these shifters are shrouded in mystery, but they're determined to protect their mates from any harm that comes their way.

Also available in audio!

Hunting Season

On the Prowl

Detyen Warriors

Detya was destroyed a hundred years ago. These doomed warriors are out to find justice... and their mates.

The Detyen Warriors series brings you kick butt heroines, alpha alien heroes, fated mates, and relationships strong enough to span the galaxy!

The entire series is also available in audio!

Soulless

Ruthless

Heartless

Faultless

Endless

Alien Holiday Romance

Christmas… in space????

These alien holiday romances look beyond Earth's winter holidays and ring in the season across the galaxy! *Select titles available in audio*.

Snowed in with the Alien Beast

The Alien's Winter Gift

The Alien Reindeer's Wild Ride

Trapped with her Alien Mate

Alien Outlaws

Outlaws, schemes, and love… it's all there in the Alien Outlaws series…

Andie Munster is sick of life on Ixilta, the planet she got dumped on after being abducted from Earth six years ago. And when the mysterious and dangerous Xandr shows up looking for a way off the planet, she's half-prisoner, half-co-conspirator in a wild rush to escape.

Rogue Alien's Escape

Rogue Alien's Woman

Rogue Alien's Secret

Rogue Alien's Legacy

Mated to the Alien

Fated Mate Alien Romance

Detyens are doomed to die young if they don't find their fated mates.

Follow along as these mated pairs fight off aliens, corrupt dictators, prejudiced humans, pirates, and more! The books can be read or listened to in any order, though some characters show up in multiple stories.

Select books available in audio.

Pick a book and jump into the action today!

Ruwen

Tyral

Stoan

Cyborg

Krayter

Kayleb

Shayn

Braxtyn

Doryan

Dekon

Stealing the Alpha

The thief takes what she wants, but the alpha keeps what's his...

Join shifter thief Mel as she clashes with lion alpha Luke in an explosive trilogy of two opposites who can't keep away from one another.

Also available in audio!

The Alpha Heist

Entangled with the Thief

In the Alpha's Bed

Save with box sets!

Aliens. Shifters. Warriors. Mates. Get them all wrapped together in these special box sets. Save up to 30% off the price of buying the individual books, depending on the series!

Alien Outlaws: The Complete Series

Mated to the Alien Volume One (also available in audio)

Mated to the Alien Volume Two (also available in audio)

Mated to the Alien Volume Three

Mated to the Alien Volume Four

Stealing the Alpha: The Complete Series (also available in audio)

The Mate Bundle

Detyen Warriors Volume One (also available in audio)

Detyen Warriors Volume Two (also available in audio)

Standalone Paranormal and Sci-Fi Romance:

Crashed

Mated on the Moon

Mated to the Alien Dragon

Marked

Bear in Mind

Alpha's Mercy

Gemma's Mate

Find more by Kate Rudolph at www.katerudolph.net

ABOUT KATE RUDOLPH

Kate Rudolph is a paranormal and alien romance author who lives in Indiana. She loves writing about kick butt heroines and the steamy heroes who love them. She's been devouring romance novels since she was too young to be reading them and had to hide her books so no one would take them away. She couldn't imagine a better job in this world than writing romances and sharing them with her fellow readers.

If you enjoyed this story, please consider leaving a review.